Arthur Helps

Ivan de Biron

Or, the Russian court in the middle of last century. Vol. 1

Arthur Helps

Ivan de Biron
Or, the Russian court in the middle of last century. Vol. 1

ISBN/EAN: 9783337297527

Printed in Europe, USA, Canada, Australia, Japan

Cover: Foto ©Raphael Reischuk / pixelio.de

More available books at **www.hansebooks.com**

IVAN DE BIRON

OR, THE RUSSIAN COURT IN THE MIDDLE
OF LAST CENTURY

BY THE

AUTHOR OF " FRIENDS IN COUNCIL," ETC.

IN THREE VOLUMES
VOL. I.

W. ISBISTER & CO.
56, LUDGATE HILL, LONDON
1874

PRINTED BY TAYLOR AND CO.,
LITTLE QUEEN STREET, LINCOLN'S INN FIELDS.

CONTENTS OF VOLUME I.

BOOK I.

BOOK II.

BOOK I.

BOOK I.

CHAPTER I.

DESCRIPTION OF THE STATE OF AFFAIRS AT THE
RUSSIAN COURT, A.D. 1740.

ON the 18th of October, 1740, Mr. Finch, the English Ambassador at St. Petersburg, sent a despatch to Lord Harrington, then Secretary of State for the Northern Department, in which were the following words :—

" The Empress Anne died in the night of the 17th of October ; the end of her life having been attended with such exquisite torments, that even those who had the greatest interest in her preservation, could only pray to God for her being delivered from so much misery. The Princesses Elizabeth and Anne took leave of her two hours before her death; the Duke of Courland was with her to her end."

The Princess Elizabeth was the daughter of Peter the Great and Catharine the First. As, however, Peter's wife and Catharine's husband were alive at the time when the Princess Elizabeth was born, her legitimate claims to the throne were very small; and, during the two preceding reigns, she had been passed over in the succession.

The Princess Anne was the granddaughter of Peter's elder brother. She had recently been married to Anthony Ulric, Grand Duke of Brunswick. They were a young couple, the Grand Duke being twenty-four years, and his Duchess twenty-two years, of age. A child had been born to them, named Ivan, who was but two months old at the date of the death of the Empress Anne, announced in the foregoing extract of the despatch to the Court of St. James's.

It may here be mentioned that Peter the
Great had arrogated to himself and his succes-
sors the privilege of naming the person in the
Imperial family who should succeed to the
throne, independently of the claims of heirship.

Mr. Finch, in subsequent passages of his despatch, declares that "all is quiet at St. Petersburg; and that everything looks prosperous for
the new *régime.*" We may conclude, however,
with the historian Von Raumer, that this glow-
ing account of the state of things at the Russian
Court was meant to be read by the Authorities.
There were other parts of the despatch written
in cypher, which might have told a different tale.
At any rate, a different tale was to be told at the
time when the despatch reached the Court of
St. James's.

It was on the very day that Mr. Finch's
letter was placed in the hands of Lord Harrington, that in a room of the Summer Palace of
St. Petersburg, there sat a young man busily
engaged writing at a table covered with maps
and papers. This young man's name was Ivan

de Biron, and he was the private Secretary of
John Ernest de Biron, Duke of Courland, the
newly appointed Regent of Russia.   Raised
from a low condition, the son of a Master-huntsman, and the grandson of a groom, the Duke*
had been the favourite of the late Empress
Anne.   For the last eight years of her reign,
he had been her principal Minister; and his
government had been distinguished by its
vigour, its sternness, and its implacable severity
during the whole of that period.   No fewer than
ten thousand human beings were languishing in
exile in Siberia, victims to his suspicious temper
and cruel disposition.

   The last will of the Empress Anne declared as
her successor Ivan the Third, an infant of two

---

   * Throughout this narrative the Duke of Courland is
called *Biron*. His family name was *Biren* or *Bühren*. The
groom and the master-huntsman, his grandfather and his
father, had been contented with that mode of spelling the
family name; but when the Duke rose to power, it was discovered that the Birens were connections of the renowned
Ducs de Biron in France; and, accordingly, the Regent
wrote his name Biron.

months old, the son, as before stated, of Anthony
Ulric, Duke of Brunswick, and of Anne the
granddaughter of Peter the Great's elder brother.

In 'a clause of the same will, the Empress
Anne confided the Regency of Russia to the
Duke of Courland, whose powers were to continue in force until Ivan the Third should be
seventeen years of age.

Such was the state of things when our story
commences. The Duke's private Secretary
before-mentioned, was a young man of frank ·
demeanour and of prepossessing appearance.
Any observer of physiognomy, however, could
not but have noticed the expression of mingled
fear, mistrust, and weariness which seemed to
have taken possession, as it were, of the young
man's countenance. And if such an observer
had gone into the adjacent rooms, he could not
but have seen that, in a lesser degree, the same
expression sat upon the faces of the numerous
secretaries, under-secretaries, and clerks, who
formed the official establishment of the all-
powerful Duke-Regent of Russia. It was no

easy task to execute the orders of such a man
as Biron, who demanded not only obedience and
fidelity, but the strictest acquiescence and ap-
proval. The slightest murmur or objection on
the part of any one of his retainers, might be
the first step on the road to Siberia for that ill-
advised individual.

The thoughts of the Private Secretary, occasionally expressed in words, ran thus :—" More
arrests; more orders for exile ; more work for
·the executioner ;—and when will my turn come ?
They pay court to me, the slaves, because I am
related to him. They do not see that I am but
a hostage in his hands for the good behaviour of
his relations, whom he hates and fears as much
as he does the rest of the world. What if I
were to forge a passport for myself, and fly ?
But no : there is the Princess Marie. I may yet
do something to render her exile less miserable.
Little she knows who would give his life to save
hers."

Who was the Princess Marie, and how was it
that Ivan de Biron was so much interested in

her that his care for her welfare should be a sufficient inducement to stay him in the design which
he was, otherwise, almost inclined to adopt—to
quit the service of the Duke of Courland, and
seek peace and safety in some other country than
Russia ?

The Princess Marie Andréevna was the only
daughter of a certain Prince Serbatoff, who had
served officially in several departments of the
State. He had, however, the misfortune of
being nearly connected with the Dolgorouckis, a
family most hateful to the Duke of Courland.
On their downfall, Prince Serbatoff had been
involved in their ruin, and had been banished to
Siberia. His daughter, Marie, had previously
been presented at Court, and had been
one of the young ladies who, from her beauty
and her wit, had attracted the observation of all
the young men who had the privilege of attending the Court balls and festivities given by the
late Empress Anne.

Ivan de Biron, as the Secretary to the Duke of
Courland, attended his master, and was present

at these festivities. From his comparatively
humble rank, he had enjoyed no opportunities
of addressing, or even approaching his idol; but
he had worshipped her from a distance; and to
him, there was no one to be compared to the
Princess Marie Andréevna Serbatoff.

To his romantic nature, it was peculiarly delightful to think, that, obscure as he was, he
could do her more service than any of her grand
admirers among the highest classes; and he had
constituted himself, unknown to her, or to any
of her family, as their protector. It was, at the
present moment, the main object of his life,
secretly to befriend them. Whatever comfort or
consolation could be provided on the journey of
the Serbatoffs to Siberia, had been provided by
the loving watchfulness of Ivan; and now he
could not forego the opportunity, which his near
relationship and official proximity to the Duke of
Courland gave him, of mitigating the misery in
exile of this family, and perhaps of restoring
them to their previous position in the State.

Ivan was still absorbed in thought when the

Regent suddenly entered the room—a stern-looking, handsome, commanding man, about fifty-four years of age. The most remarkable thing to be noticed in the expression of his countenance was, that craft seemed there to struggle with passion, and to have been superinduced upon it. A similar trait was noticeable in all that he said and did. Sometimes he spoke with exceeding suavity : sometimes the natural fierceness of his soul broke out in tones and language of resistless severity. His greeting of his Private Secretary was on this occasion very suave and graciously familiar.

" Ivan, dear child, (what a fortunate youth to have the same name as his sovereign !) Ivan, my dear, are the despatches for Denmark and England ready—those announcing my Regency ? "

" Yes, your Highness, they are."

Then came a question in a very different tone. " Are the orders to the Commandant of Schlüsselberg for the reception of those wretches prepared ? "

" Yes, your Highness, they are here."

The Regent then sat down, and began to sign
the various letters and orders that were brought
to him by the Secretary.

Suddenly, a noise outside of joyful exclamation
was heard.   The Regent started.   " Go to the
window," he said, " see what fools are there. We
cannot be disturbed now.   These hired plaudits
do not delight me.   You should stop them,
Ivan."

The Secretary went to the window, and timidly
announced that the Field Marshal, Count Münnich, was coming across the Grand Square ; and
that the soldiers of the guard, and some of the
citizens, were receiving him with shouts of applause.

" Ha ! it was for him, then, was it ? " said the
Regent, as he went on signing the papers. After
a minute or two, he added, " What regiment is
on duty to day ? "—a question which boded no
good to that regiment. Before, however, the
Secretary could answer the question, the Field-
Marshal was announced, and had entered the
room.

Great as was then that man's renown, it is necessary now to explain who he was, and how he had gained that renown.   It would mightily have astonished most men in that age, and no one more than his somewhat vain and arrogant self, that there should be this necessity : for his fame was European.

Marshal Münnich was born in 1683, in the Duchy of Oldenburg. His ancestors were noble ; but their chief distinction was to be found in the fields of science rather than of war. A genius for mathematics and skill in engineering were hereditary in the Münnich family; and the Field Marshal had a full share of these hereditary talents.

At the early age of sixteen, he commenced his career as a soldier.   He served with credit under Marlborough, and was present at the battle of Ramilies.   Afterwards he took service with Prince Eugène, and accompanied that great commander throughout his campaigns in Italy and Flanders.

Münnich then chose Russia as his field of

action; but, at first, found no favour with Peter
the Great. The refined manners of the young
German were repellent to the hard nature and
coarse habits of the Czar.

That shrewd employer, however, soon discovered the singular capacity which Münnich
had for hydraulic engineering; and the Emperor
entrusted to him the conduct of his greatest
civil enterprize—the formation of the Canal of
Ladoga. On his deathbed, the Czar derived
some comfort from hearing of the progress of
the works at Ladoga; and he must have been
satisfied with the engineer, for he exclaimed,
" *J'espère que les travaux de Münnich me
gueriront* "— a hope that was not to be fulfilled.

Peter's widow, Catharine, pressed on the
works at Ladoga; but she did not live to see
them completed. That peaceful triumph was
reserved for the reign of the Empress Anne.
Under this Czarina, Münnich resumed his career
as a soldier, and became the greatest general
that Russia possessed at that period. Indeed,

there were military men in other countries, who
did not hesitate to place him in the same rank
as Prince Eugène and Marlborough.

By this time Münnich had gained the bâton of
a Field Marshal, and had recently led the Russian armies to victory over both the Turks and
the Tartars. He had defeated the renowned
Seraskier, Vely Bashaw; had passed the Pruth
under the fire of the enemy; and had forced
the skilfully-designed and well-defended lines
of Perecop.

He was very handsome, had great dignity of
presence, and a commanding stature. During his
severest campaigns, he had shared the fatigues
and the privations of the common soldiers; and
had shown a hardihood that surpassed their
own.

Like many great commanders, Münnich was
haunted and deluded by the idea that his genius
was as potent in civil as in military affairs. One
qualification, held in those times to be very
needful for statesmanship, he certainly did possess—a wonderful power of dissimulation. But

he was too changeful a man to pursue, for any
lengthened period, great designs of policy; and
his habits of military command sometimes prevented judicious management on his part, either
of his colleagues, or of his subordinates in civil
life. He was shrewd, brave, witty, resolute, and
very fertile in resource. His chief failing was a
certain restless impatience; and this was dis-
cernible in his mobile countenance and in his
eager, demonstrative gestures.

As the Field Marshal entered the room, the
Private Secretary, Ivan de Biron, rose to leave
it. Before he could do so, the Duke said to
him in a marked manner, " I shall want to have
an answer to the question which I asked just
now. You may go."

Ivan bowed, and withdrew.

BOOK I.

———

CHAPTER II.

THE two great personages, who principally ruled Russia at this moment, were thus face to face. There was a third potentate, the Grand Chamberlain, Count Ostermann; but he ruled men from his sick chamber which he rarely left. On every great occasion, whenever there was a crisis in the fortunes of the Russian Court or Empire, Count Ostermann was suddenly seized with a fresh accession of illness. This would increase to absolute prostration, rendering him totally unable to be present when dangerous questions.

VOL. I.   C

were before the Council of State, and when compromising papers had to be signed by the councillors.

The Regent received the Field Marshal with the utmost graciousness of manner. Had not this devoted friend urged upon the Regent to take the Regency as a solemn duty to his adopted country, Russia; and had not Münnich even knelt or offered to do so, in order to persuade him? The shrewd Ambassador, who at that time represented England at the Court of St. Petersburg, had, in his despatch of the 21st of October, given his Government a description of the scene, in the course of which description, he hinted that Biron's reluctance to accept the Regency was like the unwillingness of an ecclesiastic to accept a bishopric, and it might be summed up in the words *nolo episcopari*. On the other hand, there is good reason for thinking that Biron did not accept this great office without some reluctance, foreseeing the possibility of much danger to himself. Up to this time, however, everything had gone most prosperously with the new Regent.

The Field Marshal responded to the gracious manner of the Regent by an air of obsequious deference and affection.   There is no doubt, though, that these two confederates, who had practically made the will for the dying Empress —a will which she had signed reluctantly, fully appreciating the danger for her favourite—were not such good friends as they had been a few days before.   They had not exactly quarrelled over the spoil; but their interests were beginning to diverge.   The Regent, who had spies everywhere, knew that the Field Marshal paid frequent visits—visits not always mentioned to him by his friend—to the Winter Palace, where the father and mother of the infant Emperor resided with the child.   As was natural, their views and wishes were adverse to the Regent's; and, doubtless, the mother of the infant Emperor, the Grand Duchess of Brunswick, thought that the Regency should have been entrusted to her.

The two statesmen had a long conference. At first, they talked of matters in which they

c 2

were jointly concerned, such as the instructions to be given to the Regent's representatives at foreign Courts, and the distribution of various offices which were vacant, or were to be made vacant.

The Regent, in his most subdued and gentle manner, changed the topic of the conversation.

"And now, Duke," he said, "about your own affairs?"

"Your Highness," replied Münnich, "honours me with a title to which I have no claim."

"Yes, I forgot," rejoined the Regent; "but you will see why the word was in my mind. And," he added smiling, "it has sometimes, I think, been in yours. At least it ought to have been; for I do not know of any one who has such claims to the Dukedom of the Ukraine as yourself. I spoke to the late Empress more than once about it. You are not a mere soldier, however great in that capacity—forgive a civilian for thinking that even a renowned general may be a mere soldier—but you would govern that recent conquest, so that it would be a real accession to the Empire. I am sure of that.''

This appeal to the vanity of the Field Marshal was not, for the moment, without some effect ; but he thought to himself that if the Regent had but spoken to the late Empress favourably, both the title and the appanage of the Ukraine would long ago have been conceded to him. It was true that they had been distinct and expressed objects of his ambition.

"This may be a subject," he replied, "for further consideration, and a mark of your Highness's favour at some future period. At present—"

The Regent interrupted him, and said, "That was exactly, Münnich, what I was coming to. The Grand Duchess and her silly little husband may object now; but I have news to tell you of a matter, which, if made good use of, may ensure our object. There are disturbances on the south-eastern frontier. The hill tribes are in arms again ; and these troubles have, in part, extended to the Ukraine ; and will, no doubt, extend still

further. I know it would not be worth while,
even to assure the security of the Empire in that
direction, for such a man as you are, to take the
command in person of the operations there,
but—"

Here the Field Marshal interrupted.

" No, certainly not."

" These disturbances, Münnich, are of more
moment than may at first appear. Recollect
that the death of the late Empress was almost
sudden, and certainly was unexpected either by
the Court physicians or myself. It finds us
somewhat unprepared. Then the nomination of
that infant to the throne, not that it could
wisely have been otherwise, and the comparative
feebleness of the Regency, which, as you know,
my dear friend, you forced upon me, render any
such outbreaks no slight matter.

" It is only a thing to laugh at, a playing of
babies at conspiracy; but still, you know, one
could not let it go on—I mean that idiotcy of the
Grand Duke's. Some day, Münnich, that little
sinner may find accomplices of somewhat higher

rank and more statecraft than the Court-coach-
man's buffoon, a young apprentice, and a waiter
at an inn—three of the wise heads which
his Highness took into his councils the other
day, when he was minded a little to rebel.
Greater men than these might join him.   Eh!
Münnich ? "

During this somewhat long address, the Field
Marshal had looked fixedly at the Regent, whose
eyes had fallen beneath that steadfast gaze.
There was afterwards silence for a minute or
two; and then the Field Marshal said slowly
but emphatically,

"I should be very reluctant to leave your
Highness at this juncture.   What you have just
said confirms that feeling."

"There is no solid ground for fear as yet,"
replied the Regent; "but there will be in the
future.   That insolent Scotchman, Keith, has
addressed his soldiery in terms that bode no
good to either of us.   He will be true, forsooth,
to his infant Czar, but does not condescend to
recognize Our Regency, and will take no oath to
us.   You doubtless hate the man as I do."

The Regent, as he said this, had quite lost his mellifluous tones of speech, but he regained them as he continued the conversation.

" For the present, I can take care of myself, but I shall want all your aid, hereafter, to keep these Generals of division in order. Not to gain fresh laurels—that would be too absurd—but to effect our object, I think it would be wise for you to proceed at once to the frontier of the Ukraine. In a few brief months you will have composed these troubles, and have added fresh claims to honour and reward—fresh claims in a new reign, mark you. That pompous little potentate, the Duke of Brunswick, would claim for himself the title of Generalissimo ; but when you come back, there would be no doubt as to who should have supreme command over the armies and the fleets of Russia. And, in the meanwhile, the patent for the Dukedom of the Ukraine could be made out for you on the news of your first success reaching us."

The Regent, as before indicated, was not a real proficient in the art of dissimulation—only a forward pupil. Certain nervous movements in his countenance betrayed his anxiety as to whether his purpose was concealed, and whether the restless Field Marshal would fall into the snare thus, with little adroitness, prepared for him. Count Münnich, on the contrary, was an accomplished dissembler. He appreciated the full danger of his position, and thoroughly understood the anxiety of the Regent to be well rid of him for the present. He finally, however, made no objection to the Regent's proposal. Further advices, he thought, might perhaps be waited for; and some preparation must be made; but no doubt his good friend was right. He did not deny that it had been his ambition, at one time of his life, to be named as General-issimo; but now he thought the claims of the father of the Emperor were pre-eminent. All that he wished for, was the security of the Regency to his friend.

Before they parted, the Regent expressed his hope that the Field Marshal saw the Imperial family frequently and gave them good advice, as he was sure he would do. For his own part, the immense amount of pressing business which had devolved upon him in the last few days, had prevented his paying his respects as frequently to the great people at the Winter Palace as he could have wished.

"Moreover, I am not sure," he said, "that I should have been very welcome; for I have been obliged to read that foolish Duke some severe lessons, which I have chiefly done by writing to the Grand Duchess."

The Field Marshal then took his leave, being honoured by a fraternal embrace from the Regent, as was the custom in that country at that time.

In an hour afterwards, Count Münnich was closeted with the Grand Duchess; this time having entered the Winter Palace in the disguise of a major's uniform.

BOOK I.

—◆—

CHAPTER III.

THE REGENT'S MEDITATION AFTER MÜNNICH'S DEPARTURE — DESCRIPTION OF BIRON'S PLANS, EDUCATION, AND AIMS.

THE Regent remained for some time absorbed in thought. No one looking at him now, could have imagined that this man had reached the highest pinnacle of fortune to which any subject could aspire. It is true that one of his schemes had been to gain the succession to the Empire for one of his own descendants by the intermarriage of his children with those of the Imperial family. The late Empress Anne, though

dotingly attached to the Duke, and very sub-
servient to him, for, as it is said, she had often
knelt at his feet to dissuade him from his cruel
prosecutions of real or supposed enemies, could
not brook the idea of the grandchildren or great-
grandchildren of a groom, inheriting the throne
of Russia. In everything but that scheme, Biron
had succeeded. The potent influence of Russia
had given to this adventurer the Duchy of Courland; and he had been, for some years, an
independent and Sovereign Prince. And now,
too, within the last few days, he had become,
practically speaking, the Sovereign of Russia.
There are few instances of a man, with such
small claims for eminence, at least as regards
birth or station, having risen to such a height of
fortune. Vast revenues he already possessed,
still greater revenues had been pressed upon him
to support his dignity as Regent. He had entirely verified, and acted up to a saying which
those who had been his friends at college remembered to have often heard him make use of,—
namely, " *Il se faut pousser au monde,*" or, as it

was expressed to those who did not know French,
"*Man muss fein suchen, sich in der Welt empor
zu bringen.*" But, as the person upon whose
authority this saying of the young Biron is given,
adds, "Fortune turns upon hinges" (*Das Glück
ist angelrund.*)

More wretched individuals might have been
found in the Empire of Russia than its Regent,
the Duke of Courland,—the miserable families,
for instance, whom he had driven into exile in
Siberia; but, probably, at that moment, there
was not one human being in that huge Empire
whose soul was more shaken and disordered by
fears, doubts, suspicions, and apprehensions, than
that of the Sovereign Minister.

It is a fond fashion of the world, and it is a
comfort to most men's vanity, to make out that
those whom they call the favourites of fortune,
owe all to fortune, and little or nothing to merit.
This is rarely the case, and certainly was not so
with the Duke of Courland. On the accession of
the late Empress, he was merely her Chamberlain,
a personal favourite; but he distinctly foresaw,

that the government of the Empire would fall
into his hands. And he prepared himself for it.
Abstaining for two years from all direct inter-
ference with public affairs, he devoted himself to
those studies which should fit him for a statesman. Though of mean extraction, he had been
educated at Königsberg; and so careful a
thinker could not fail to apply some of the knowledge which he had acquired at that seat of
learning. He had always been a lover of books,
and had formed one of the greatest and most
valuable libraries collected by any private person
during that century. Moreover, he had favoured
learned men, and had sought companionship with
them. It is not improable, that, at this moment
of his career, the fate of Sejanus was present to
his mind, and he was well aware that if he should
fall, it would afford the keenest delight to the
people whom, according to the measure of his
intelligence, he had faithfully served, whose
material interests he had carefully maintained
and improved, but over whom he had tyrannized
with inflexible severity, looking upon his enemies as the enemies of the State.

After a long meditation, the Regent sprang from his seat suddenly, saying to himself, "I will see whether the piquets are stationed in the streets at the points where I ordered them to be; and, perhaps, I may hear what my good people are pleased to say of their Regent."

"Ivan."

At his master's call, the Secretary entered.

"What regiment is it?"

The Secretary told him.

"A faithful set of fellows," said the Regent, in his most mellifluous tones. "We could trust them to guard our State prisoners at Schlüsselberg, I think. Inform the Minister of War that their services will be required at that fortress, and that one of the regiments, now stationed there, may return.

"Good fellows, excellent fellows, Ivan, but noisy."

BOOK I.

——◆——

CHAPTER IV.

THE GYPSIES—THE REGENT IN DISGUISE HEARS HIS
FORTUNE—SONGS.

OF all the inhabitants of the great Empire of Russia, if indeed, we can call nomads inhabitants, the gypsies led at that time the happiest life. No statesman, even when most suspicious, connected them with any Court intrigue. They wandered about from province to province, living well upon the fears and hopes of the most credulous persons of a most superstitious and credulous community; and, with a view to gain some groundwork for their wizard skill, the gypsies took care to be well acquainted with the secret history of all that was going on.

The celebrated Russian poet Poushkin has given a vivid description of gypsy life :—

> "An unruly band of gypsies" (so the poem commences)
>   wander through Bessarabia,
> They pass the night beneath coarse tents close to the river
>   side,
> Such a night's lodging is as sweet as liberty itself,
> The carts and kibitkas have carpet-covered hoods ;
> Between the wheels, burn fires,
> Around which each family prepares its supper.
> The horses are grazing in the field,
> A tame bear lies free behind the carts,
> All is life and freedom."

He afterwards describes their journey the next morning.

> "The asses bear the playful children in their panniers :
> Husbands, brothers, wives, and maidens follow.
> What screaming and riot !
> The songs of the gypsies, and the roaring of the bear im-
>   patiently rattling his chain ;
> The variety of the coloured rags, the half nakedness of the
>   children,
> The barking and howling of the dogs,
> The noise of the bag-pipes, and the rattling of the carts,

All is poverty, wildness, and confusion,
But full of movement and life.
What a contrast to our dead effeminacy,
To that frivolous and idle life of ours—
A life monotonous as the songs of slaves ! "*

At this eventful period in Russian history, an unusual number of gypsies were in St. Petersburg. Any change of surrounding circumstances is favourable to these people; and it was known to them, even before it was surmised by the great personages at Court, that the Empress Anne's disorder was a mortal one. Little else that had since occurred, whether amongst the populace or at Court, had escaped their attention and their unbounded curiosity.

On the evening of that day, in the early part of which the Regent and the Field Marshal had held a conference, fated to have so great an influence on the fortunes of both of them, a troop of these gypsies were singing their songs, and telling fortunes, in the " Italian Garden," (what a misnomer !) at the eastern end of the town. It was

---

* " The Russians at Home," Sutherland Edwards.

becoming dusk, but there was still light enough to discern the countenances of those who approached to have their fortunes told.

The Russians are a most musical people, destined, as some think, to succeed to the inheritance of the Germans in the musical expression both of the tenderest and the most sublime ideas.

The gypsies had accommodated themselves to the tastes of the people amongst whom they dwelt, and had not failed, when in Russia, to cultivate their musical powers to the utmost.

They now sang a song of a mournful character, which was a great favourite with the Russians. The following is a prose version; but the full effect of the words can hardly be appreciated except by one who has traversed the vast forests of some northern climate, and is familiar with the phenomenon which the song describes.

There is a sound in the forest.
It is not the weary waving of the branches storm-swept;
It is not the hurrying to and fro of the brown autumn
    leaves;

It is not the far-off howling of the wild beasts of the
forest;
It is not the humming of the little things with many eyes
and feet.
It is not the music of the birds when they meet in their
groves, contending in song.
It is the great imprisoned spirit of the wood,
He ever and ever moans, until he can mingle with the free
spirits of the upper air;
Ever and ever,
Ever and ever he moans,

After the song had ended, and the chief of the
band of gypsies had announced that the decrees
of fate would now be told to any one who had the
courage and the wisdom to listen to them, several
claimants stepped forward to enjoy this high
privilege of learning, not only their own fortunes,
but the fortune of the world in which they lived.
For in no lesser pride of prophetic knowledge had
the chief of the gypsies announced their high
claim to distinct intelligence of the unknown
future.

Among the claimants who thus came forward,
were several young men. It is probable that the

wide knowledge of human affairs which had been promised, did not possess so much interest for them as their own peculiar fortunes. The gypsy chief, by nodding to one of them, signified the choice he had made. This chosen one had somewhat of a grave and serious countenance, and there was a look of anxiety in it. Perhaps this was the reason why he was chosen, for nothing puzzles and perplexes a soothsayer more than having a vacant and inexpressive countenance to deal with. The young man in question had come forward reluctantly, and had even been pushed to the front by an elder man who was his companion.

The gypsy chief, after he had made his choice of the youth whose fortune was to be told, indicated by an imperious gesture that person of their tribe who was to tell it. This was a young girl who came out of the circle with somewhat of a shy manner, and advanced towards the young man with an uncertain and hesitating step, as if she loved not publicity of any kind.

As this maiden afterwards becomes a most

important person in this story, it may be well to
describe her appearance here.   She was small in
stature, and delicate in feature.   Her complexion
resembled that of her swarthy companions, without being quite so dark as theirs ; but there was
a great and singular difference from them in the
colour of her hair and of her eyes.   These were
not dark.   The hair was of the very deepest
chestnut colour ; the eyes were of a colour for
which there is no name, at any rate in our language.   This is not to be wondered at ; for, in
traversing the streets of any great capital for
many hours in the course of any day, you will
probably not meet with more than two or three
persons whose eyes are of the colour sought to be
described.   The nearest approach to description
which can be given of this colour is, that it is
what you would imagine would be presented by
a transparent grey with a dark colour behind
it.

Altogether, the girl was most beautiful ; and
the singularity of her appearance was not so
marked as to detract from that beauty.   She had

an exquisitely formed hand and arm; and this beauty had been but slightly marred by the hard toil which generally fell to the lot of the women of her tribe. Her name was Azra.

As she laid her small, brown plump hand in that of the young man; and without looking at it, felt for the lines in it which were to instruct her so certainly about his future fortunes, he could not but notice the remarkable beauty of her features.

What she said to him was not heard by the bystanders. It spoke of a fair young lady (the young man smiled), not very fair; indeed her eyes were dark, and she was proud, and he who loved her had many hopes and more fears. There was a line in his hand which betokened sorrow for this year; but the line of victory was so deep and strong that it must overcome all obstacles. There would be great rejoicings, and he was one who would have much cause to rejoice, on the next inundation but one of the Neva.

Her tale was told; but before the young man and the maiden parted, their eyes met, and there

was an arch look in the gipsy girl's countenance
and a gesture of her hands which were inter-
preted by the young man to mean, " All this I tell
you much as I tell the rest of the youths: it is
my trade and you may put what faith you like in
my sayings. Mayhap there is some truth in
them after all."

Thus Ivan de Biron construed the look, for he
it was who, having as it seemed but little to do,
had come out to have his fortune told. It was a
day when most of the official persons in Russia
would have been very glad to have been informed what was to happen to them, considering
the critical state of political affairs.

There then stepped forward to have his fortune
told, a person of a very different semblance
from Ivan de Biron, though he had come with
him as a companion. He was a man of middle
height, with an expression of countenance half
anxious, half contemptuous, who mockingly desired his fortune to be told. He was dressed in
sober fashion, and looked like the steward of a
great household, who had many servants to look

after, and much wealth to regulate. He appeared to be endeavouring to look humble; but if he aimed at doing so, his aim signally failed.

The other persons who wished to have their fortunes told, gave way to him at once, and whispered to one another "that they were sure they should be knouted if they interfered with him."

Azra was about to take his hand, and to exercise the ordinary craft of gypsies, when there suddenly broke out a sort of choral song, the burden of which in the language of the gypsies was—"It is he, it is he; the ruler of horses and the ruler of men."

The chief made a signal to Azra to withdraw; and an aged gypsy woman was substituted in her stead. The seeming steward placed a gold piece in the old woman's hand. She led him aside while the gypsies continued their song. She looked into his hand and then into his eyes; and, in a familiar manner, which he shrank from, smoothed down his cheeks with her coarse wrinkled hands. Then, lifting up the forefinger of her left hand, she said, " I see a palace, and I see a hut; and the snow lies in heaps round that hut, and the snowy mountains are in the far distance; and there are bars to the windows of the hut; and the reindeer gallops by at night; and the wolves are hunting down their prey; and all is desolate and all is silent. The ghosts dance by moonlight on the plains before the hut; and a man looks out and sees them; and there is no peace for him, for they are the ghosts of those who were his enemies."

The steward smiled and said, "Ghosts, my mother, are feeble creatures, and a brave man mocks at them." And she replied, "There is one thing he cannot mock at, and that is night. The white-handed love the night; but let him beware of night." And then she shrieked out the words "Night, night, night," and the chorus of the gypsies took up the refrain.

The grave man withdrew from the crowd, and made his way homewards, alone, for he had given no sign to his companion to accompany him, and the young man respectfully abstained

from intruding his company upon the elder.
That home was the Summer Palace; and though
he entered the building with a certain grave
humility, as became a steward of the household, yet all the sentinels seemed to wish to
present arms to him, and one of them did so,
but his salute was not acknowledged. The
seeming steward, when once he had entered the
palace, walked through its corridors as if they
belonged to him, and gained his chamber.
When there, he had no rest, but kept constantly
repeating to himself the words "night, night,
night;" and he said to himself, "They are a
miserable people, these gypsies, but they know
the secrets of men; and the hearts of fools are
wide open to them. In three days at furthest,
Münnich shall leave St. Petersburg, and bestir
himself to compose the troubles at the frontier."

BOOK I.

———

CHAPTER V.

IT was early on the day after the Field
Marshal's interview with the Regent that he
sent for his Adjutant-General, Manstein, whom
he greeted in a very warm and cordial manner.

"Brother and comrade in arms," he said, "a
glorious future is before us. The tribes on the
south-eastern frontier are troublesome, and it will
be our duty to compel them to obedience. My
generals, who have so often led their divisions
into victory, will now crown their noble efforts

by bringing order and discipline into these rude tribes.   I myself am to accompany the army, and thus to gain fresh laurels."

Manstein thought he knew his commander well.   He had been for many years his favourite, and one of his most trusted officers.   He knew full well the versatility of the man he had to deal with; but the present mood of the Field Marshal was one the like of which he had never known.

Münnich did not fail to recognize Manstein's astonishment and even disgust, but continued in the same strain, "What was the passing of the Pruth, what was our forcing the lines of Perekop, compared with the exploits that are now before us?   It is true" (and here the Field Marshal sneered bitterly) "that the names of these barbarian leaders are not quite so well known to the world as that of the Seraskier Vely Bashaw; but the world's opinion of the greatness of exploits is not always a just one."

Here Manstein ventured to interpose, "I grant the need, my lord, of suppressing revolt wherever it may threaten; but could not one of your

generals be entrusted with the enterprise.   Must
the Field Marshal, the first soldier in Russia, be
there in person?"

"Why, Manstein, so the great man wills it.
I hardly think, indeed, that if the Field Marshal
were not to be there in person, our crafty
Regent's mind would be so disturbed at these
possible dangers on the frontier."

"But now, my lord, when all is unsettled, the
Empire new, St. Petersburg itself so dubious in
fidelity that there are piquets in the streets, and
the city is almost in a state of siege—surely,
your leaving the capital would be madness."

"Of course it would—madness as regards the
safety of the child-Emperor and the Grand
Duchess; but not so for the Regent.   My trusted
friend," said Münnich suddenly changing his
tone, "this is the scheme of that man to remove
me, and thus to be unchecked in power.   Think
you, for a moment, that I will yield to it?"

"Ah! now," said Manstein, "my commander
speaks like himself."

"I marvel at my past folly," replied the Field

Marshal "Who that has stood in the path of
Courland has long remained to thwart him?
The way to Siberia is whitened by the bones of
his victims; but I will not be one of them.

"Do you think that I do not know the man?
He has ever been my bitterest enemy; he robbed
me of my house in former days; he kept me ever
in the background at Court. When I asked for
some reward for my great services from the late
woman, was it his speech or hers? or if hers,
surely prompted by him, that I should soon be
asking to be made Grand Duke of Muscovy?"

Manstein could not help thinking that if his
chief had all along discerned the Duke of Courland's implacable enmity against him, it was
somewhat strange that he had lately taken so
active a part in gaining for the Duke the Regency
of Russia.

The Field Marshal seemed to have divined his
thoughts, for he exclaimed with vehemence,
"Write me down as the greatest fool in this
Empire, worthy to have been summoned into
council by his Highness of Brunswick with the

coachman's buffoon, and Sergius the waiter; but
I did think that the villain could not have done
without me. We, too, Ostermann and I, have
our spies, Manstein, and have heard how he has
described us, even in the last three days,—'the
sick fox, Ostermann; the featherheaded, vain
butcher, Münnich.' Now, did I ever sacrifice
a single man of my army needlessly?"

This accusation of being reckless of the lives of
his soldiery was one often made against this
great general, and it touched him nearly. He
continued :—

"We will spring upon him, Manstein. By
night we'll do it. See that the regiment on
guard at the Summer Palace is one devoted to
us; our own if possible. There is to be a great
banquet to-morrow. Watch him well, and if
need be, we will strike the blow to-morrow
night."

"But the Grand Duchess, my lord? Unless
she joins us, it will be rebellion; and if all
accounts be true, she is a weak, vacillating
woman."

" Already, Manstein, she hates and fears him. The slights she has endured are such as have great weight with a woman's mind. I think I can persuade her: but if not, I will do the deed myself. Will you be with me ? "

" Heart and hand, my lord, even to death."

The Field Marshal expressed his gratitude warmly to Manstein, and then dismissed him, saying that he himself must at once see the Grand Duchess. He had seen her yesterday, but only in the company of the Grand Duke, " a worthy little man," he added, " but a sieve which lets all the corn run through, while it retains the chaff most carefully. Tell him that you mean to change the fashion of your beard, it is a secret he will keep religiously: tell him that you mean to cross the river by night, and the next hour the camp followers of the army will know your intention."

The character of the Princess, with whom the Field Marshal was about to seek an interview, and upon whose decision so much depended at this moment, was one not difficult to delineate.

Good-natured, indolent, averse from business, there was but little noteworthy in the character, except in one important respect. It is a great mistake, often made by men in the estimate of women, to suppose that they are incapable of friendship, at least of the friendship which men have towards persons of their own sex. Now the Grand Duchess of Brunswick had a female friend named Juliana de Mengden, to whom she was passionately attached. The friendship of our own Queen Anne for Sarah Duchess of Marlborough, and afterwards for Mrs. Masham, was poor and feeble when compared with that of the Duchess of Brunswick for her favourite. To shut herself up for days together with her infant child and with her beloved Juliana, was her chief happiness in this life. Ulric Anthony, Duke of Brunswick, a man of much worth and not without military ability (in civil affairs very imprudent), had but little influence with his wife, and in vain endeavoured to counteract the influence of the favourite. It does not appear that Juliana de Mengden busied herself with State affairs any more than her mistress did; but her casual likings, or dislikings, had the greatest weight with the Duchess; and, at this crisis, the result probably depended more upon Juliana de Mengden than upon any other person. It seems probable from various circumstances that the lively, brilliant Field Marshal was rather pleasing to the favourite. Moreover, the families of Münnich and De Mengden were connected, the Field Marshal's eldest son having married one of Juliana's sisters.

E 2

BOOK I.

———————

CHAPTER VI.

MÜNNICH'S INTERVIEW WITH THE GRAND DUCHESS.

THE Field Marshal proceeded to the Winter Palace, and asked for an audience of the Grand Duchess, which was at once accorded to him. He found her there with her ladies, and with the infant Emperor in her arms. "Is it not beautiful?" she exclaimed, pointing to the dress of the child—"a gift from the maidens of St. Petersburg to their young Czar; and it is worthy of him."

The Marshal said that the dress was beautiful; but there was a coldness in his tone which did

not escape the notice of the mother. " I do not
think, my lord, that you like children; or perhaps it is, that the great Field Marshal is not to
be touched by these vanities of dress, which you
know, my lord, please a poor mother. At some
future day, mayhap, you will be proud of him,
when the young soldier, with his great general
by his side, is reviewing those veterans whose
noble deeds and whose fidelity have secured him
the Empire."

The Marshal stepped forward till he approached the Grand Duchess closely, and then
said in a low voice, " I greatly fear that I shall
never see that day, or accompany that young
soldier whom your Highness thus pictures to
yourself as he should appear in future years.
But I would speak alone with your Highness."

Hereupon the Grand Duchess gave a sign to
the ladies, who, with the exception of Juliana de
Mengden, withdrew.

" And now, Field Marshal," exclaimed the
Duchess, " what was the meaning of your last

mysterious speech ? What evil fate threatens our darling ? ”

“ Every day that passes over his Imperial Majesty's head, brings him nearer to the time when he will be in the way of one who has never failed to remove any human being that stood in his way. Why did he wish to have the custody of the child—I mean of his Imperial Majesty ? ”

“ That I never will consent to, Münnich.”

“ I trust not, madam. Your Highness knows that man's ambition, and how he has sought to ally his base-born brood to the Imperial family. You cannot have forgotten the slights that were put upon you throughout the last reign. You cannot but see that your own just claims to the Regency were set aside for this man.”

“ I love him not,” exclaimed the Duchess, “ but I thought that the Field Marshal and the Regent were sworn friends. To be sure, you have not sung his praises so loudly during the last few days.”

“ I grieve to find,” Münnich replied, apparently changing the subject, “ that your Highness is so troubled about those hill tribes on the south-eastern frontier. For my own part, I did not think they threatened the safety of the Empire."

" What tribes? What frontier? What does he mean, Juliana? "

" We have heard nothing about hill tribes or danger to the frontier," exclaimed the favourite.

" So then it is without having taken your Highness's pleasure, that the Regent is about to dismiss me—for I call it a dismissal—me and my best generals to defend this frontier, menaced only in his imagination. Is it thus that he begins his reign, veiled under the name of Regency? No word in Council, no orders from your Highness ! "

" This is too audacious," said the Duchess.

" Indeed it is, madam."

" One by one, your Highness's faithful friends will thus be taken from you."

" But you shall not go to the frontier, Marshal."

" If not, the next thing that your Highness will hear of your faithful friend and servant, is, that he and all who love him are on the way to Siberia."

"But I shall speak to him myself."

"Speak to him!" (The Marshal smiled.) "Your Highness will but partake my fate, sooner or later, with a certainty."

"What then is to be done? Do you know, Juliana?"

The favourite, as thoroughly perplexed as her mistress, said nothing; but looked inquiringly at the Marshal.

"The fate he means for us, for all of us, for that dear child, for her (pointing to Juliana), for all who love your Highness—must be brought upon himself. And there is no time to lose, not a day, not an hour, scarcely a minute."

"I dare not do it, Münnich. How am I, a feeble woman, not versed in State affairs, to take upon myself this burden and this danger? Little as I know of this Empire—new to me— I know that the Regent's creatures hold every office, and that his will is law with them."

"They fear, but do not love him," Münnich

replied.   "Their idol, once thrown from its pedestal, would be dragged through the mud, to the joy of all beholders,—from the highest prince to the lowest peasant in Russia. Think of the thousands he has banished, and what a wealth of hatred surrounds him!   But we waste our time in talking. Let me act. On me let the whole enterprise rest. The soldiery love me. I only ask your Highness's consent to the deed, and done it shall be."

"I cannot sanction it now; can I, Juliana? My husband, too—what will he say?"

The Duchess, in an agony of doubt, rose and walked with irresolute steps about the room. The imperial infant, not accustomed to such irregular movements, began to cry. "Leave me now, my good Münnich," the Duchess exclaimed. "We will talk further of this matter."

The Field Marshal saw that it was hopeless to gain a decision from the indecisive woman at this moment. He made his obeisance; and, giving a slight sign to the favourite, left the room. She followed him, and for some minutes they walked together up and down the western corridor. There was an earnest, whispered conversation between them, which was interrupted by the voice of the Grand Duchess calling for Juliana.

Count Münnich left the palace, and his thoughts, if they had been uttered in words, would have been these : "She is the stronger of the two, or at least not the weaker. Were this Grand Duchess an Empress Catharine, or even an Empress Anne, it might not be needed. But what possible protection is there in her ? It is doubly needful that the thing be done. I will go to Manstein. Let me see. It was the 9th Regiment of Dragoons amongst whom I slept for many nights in the camp on the Pruth. I think I know every man of them."

BOOK I.

—◆—

CHAPTER VII.

BANQUET AT THE REGENT'S PALACE.

THE Regent had issued invitations for a great banquet to be held that day, at which, of course, his good friend the Field Marshal was to be an honoured guest.

The remaining hours of the day before the time when Count Münnich was to attend the banquet, were very actively employed by him. Not once did he look behind him, whether he went on foot or in his droschky, though he well knew that wherever he went, he was closely followed by the Regent's spies. But, with a feeling of despera-

tion upon him, he considered that the chief
danger now was, lest the swiftness of his preparations should not be adequate to the fixedness of
his purpose. "Besides," he said to himself, with
the shrewdness as regards minor matters that was
characteristic of the man, "they will not make
their reports until to-morrow morning ; and then
it may be too late to make them."

The hour for the banquet arrived. The preparations for it were very magnificent. The one
thing that delighted the Regent, that seemed to
comfort his gloomy soul, and even to dispel its
gloom, was splendour of all kinds. During the
reign of the late Empress every extravagance in
dress, decoration, and equipage, was carried to
its utmost height. The polite and graceful French,
great lovers of fitness in all things, were wont
to smile at this barbaric splendour, which was
often most incongruous. Even the ruder English
mocked at it, as we learn from the despatches of
our ambassador Mr. Finch, to our own Court.
But still it had a certain magnificence ; and the
various nationalities welded into the great

Russian Empire, with the corresponding variety of costume, equipage, and manner, added an appearance of romance to the scene which was wanting in the more uniform splendour of other Courts.

The Field Marshal, surrounded by a brilliant staff of officers, was received with especial honour by the Regent, who, indeed, advanced to the principal landing of the staircase to welcome his most honoured guest.   It seemed to all the company as if these two great men, the pillars of the state, as the courtiers did not omit to call them, were knit together in the firmest bonds of friendship.   But murder, or something very like it, was in the heart of each of them.

There is nothing so remarkable in man as his power of concealing mental torture.   What is unsaid is ever nearest and greatest.   The soul is beset by some hideous remorse—consuming care —warnings of disease—fear of death—rejected love—vile pecuniary distress—or the anguish of anticipated shame.   The dark thing is not merely in the back-ground : its presence never withdrawn, its grasp never wholly relaxed, it occupies the citadel of thoughts and feelings ; and all that is beyond its sway, is but out-lying and unconsidered precincts. Meanwhile the man plays his part in society as other men do : is polite, gay, affable ; and if he is really a strong and able person, is as much like his ordinary self, himself before this dark thing had any hold upon him, as it is possible to be.

Now Count Münnich had this power of fighting against and keeping under, the dire thoughts which occupied the fortress of his mind; but the Regent had not.

Great feasts are very much alike ; and it needs not to recount at large the richness of the enter-tainment, and how, after dinner had ended, there were songs and dances which might remind one of the festivals of Roman Emperors. These festivities, however, came to an end. The less favoured guests retired, while the more favoured remained, or, as it seems, returned to enjoy the pleasure and the honour of a social evening of conversation in the presence of the Regent.

He, ever anxious, as the rest of the company thought, to do honour to his much-loved guest, the Field Marshal, led the conversation, in a royal manner, to the chief exploits of Münnich's military life.

The Count, delighted to have for a topic matters which he could discuss without any reference to present politics, was eager and earnest in the recital of his great adventures; nor did he forget to dwell upon the events of his early days, especially of his imprisonment in France, at Cambrai, where the excellent Fenelon was so good and kind to him and to his fellow-prisoners. This was an era in his life to which the Field Marshal was very fond of recurring.

Meanwhile, the Regent, apparently exhausted by the fatigues of the day, was reclining on a couch with a little table before him. Suddenly, in the midst of one of the Field Marshal's most interesting narratives, the Regent interrupted him, saying, "By the way, Münnich, did you ever undertake any enterprise by night?"

Languidly up to this moment, had the Regent listened to the Marshal's rather boastful narrative, occasionally putting in the polite questions or remarks which a wearied host thinks it necessary to do, in order to show that he is not tired of his guests and of their conversation. But this time he half rose from his couch, leant on the table, and looked fixedly into the face of the Field Marshal.

The Field Marshal was certain that his conspiracy was discovered. He felt as we mostly feel in such great crises, all the powers of life flying to the centre, and as if utterance would be denied to us; but he was one of the bravest men that ever lived, and, as we have said, a perfect master of dissimulation.

In an easy manner he replied, "In the course of my time, I have been obliged to use every hour of the twenty-four for some great purpose. I do not particularly remember any signal adventure undertaken by night. All hours are

alike to me, when I have my work to do;"
and then he resumed his interesting narrative,
which told of a military exploit that had brought
him into direct conflict with the renowned
Turkish General, the Seraskier.

BOOK I.

CHAPTER VIII.

DEPARTURE OF THE GUESTS—THE REGENT'S CONVERSATION WITH HIS SECRETARY IVAN.

As the last of his guests departed, the Regent gave a sigh of relief. For some time he remained alone, giving way to the deepest melancholy. At length he summoned Ivan, his private secretary. The young man was so impressed with the attitude and bearing of the Regent, that he ventured to address him first, a liberty he had seldom presumed to take.

"Is your Highness ill?"

"Not in the body, Ivan. But all day long a

cloud of horror has surrounded me, and weighed me down—I never knew the like—and some presentiment of evil in an embodied form has been beside me at every moment. It sits by my side where I sit now."

"Oh! my Lord, 'tis but the weight of empire that oppresses you—not a single moment's quiet since the death of the Empress! The hour is late; will you not retire to rest?"

"I dread the night more than the day," replied the Regent. "Last night my dreams were horrible. The wolves that old hag talked about hunted me down; and each one bore a human face—some face I had known, some one that hated me. 'Tis an old fable, Ivan, that by some magic power you might see into the hearts and souls of other men. It is no fable. I had that power to-day. I saw into the souls of those that sat at meat with me; and who, at each pause, commenced a new song of praise to their all-powerful and all-wise Regent. But their hearts were full of malice, Ivan; and I read their minds as if they were an open book before me. Oh! how I wearied of the prate and flippant boasting of that soldier. But the man is harmless—for the present, harmless. There is but little danger from so vain a man. Nevertheless, he goes to the frontier. I will not have him near me."

Ivan's astonishment was great at this disclosure of the Regent's purposes, for the Duke was not a man given to confide in his private secretary. He did not venture to make any remark that would show that he had listened to his Highness's last words, and merely said,

"Will you not go to bed, my lord?"

"No; I will not. Come hither, Ivan; why do you stand at such a distance? Are you, too, afraid of me?"

Ivan moved a few paces nearer to his formidable master.

"Something I have done for Russia," said the Regent mournfully, "something to fulfil the schemes of that half-crazy, half-inspired man whom they call ' Peter the Great.' Come nearer, still, Ivan. One would think I was some wild beast, whom all men fear would spring upon them. I dislike you less than I do most men. You shall for the nonce be the devil's advocate. Say what you can against the soul of Biron. What has he done, that all men should hate him? Speak out, boy; it shall not harm you. Tell what they say in the streets, and what they say in their innermost chambers, when. my spies are not beside them."

An almost mortal terror seized upon poor Ivan. A great danger on either side beset him. If he should say what he thought, could he ever be forgiven by the Regent? If he did not say it, would so shrewd a man be satisfied with this reluctance and this reticence? He chose the bolder course; and falteringly spoke thus :—

" All Russia knows, your Highness, what you have done for it. Roads, bridges, cities, owe their existence to the Duke of Courland. This splendid Court reflects your love of splendour and your desire for civilization."

"I think, my good Ivan, that I have heard these words once or twice before—even as lately as from the slaves who sat at these tables and secretly wished that my food was poison. Have you nothing else to say?"

"Yes, I have. What has been the cost of all these benefits to Russia? How many thousands, not of common criminals, have died on their journey to Siberia, or are dying in those hideous wastes? They say, the people say, your Highness, and I—I say so too, 'Was it needful to purchase those benefits at this price?'"

"Defend me from the tender mercies of the young," exclaimed the Regent. "Had I but slain, by strictly legal or military slaughter, these thousands, I should have been guiltless in your eyes, my tender-hearted Ivan. What! you would have me scotch the serpents, and leave their brood to wriggle round me—their poisonous fangs undrawn? No! I have done wisely. Who thwarted me, thwarted my aims, which ever, for the good of this empire, were predominant; and he who did so was an enemy to the State, and not to me alone. 'Not common criminals!'—as if they were not infinitely worse. They have become useful colonists instead of harmful conspirators. This touches me not—say on."

"Well, then, your Highness has provoked the envy of the nobles by your magnificence. They point at your palaces; they join with those of Courland, and accuse you of private ambition."

"And think you, my good youth, that a simple citizen who bore himself humbly, and lived like some poor Boyard from the provinces, would have been feared or respected by these barbarians? Go, go. You are honest, and I like you the better for what you have said; but you speak with your wisdom of three-and-twenty years, and you know not the world in which we live.

"But stay, what are the orders to the guard?"

"That they do not parley with any one who seeks an entrance to the palace by night, but that they cut him down forthwith."

"Are the sentinels doubled?"

"They are, your Highness."

"Not that I fear. It was a dream though

that Cæsar had before they slaughtered him in
the Senate. And so they only told you, those
gypsies, of some girl you were to marry; some
rustic girl, I think, you said, Ivan—the never-
ending trash with which they tickle fools; but
to me (for grey hairs—prematurely grey—de-
mand another story) they spoke of wolves, of
nightly wolves. Some danger they must ever
threaten, and it is] safe to prophecy misfortune
to any of the sons of men. If I, too, were a
prophet or a gypsy, I should foretell misfortune
as the surest thing to happen. Marriage to you,
my boy, and the wolves to me, as being somewhat older and wiser. Oh! they know how to
suit us all." (And here the Regent laughed
loudly, but not for long.) "They knew me
though—the wretches—they knew me. And
many things they know. Go now. I like you,
and I can trust you. We will to-morrow make
out the powers for the Field Marshal; those for
him and his generals at the frontier. That
Manstein has a look I do not like—a faithful
fellow too—one that would wade through blood

to do his master's bidding. Good night, Ivan ;
dream of the fair rustic beauty whom the gypsies
promised you, good night."

Ivan left the room with an uneasy feeling, that
he should never be forgiven for the audacious
truths he had uttered that night. But still he
felt a certain gladness that he had for once said
out fully and boldly what he had long thought,
and long desired to say.

The Regent had not been many minutes
alone, when a servant entered the room, and
said, " Herr Litmann wishes to see your
Highness."

" At this hour, Fritz ? I have seen the man
once before to-day."

" I told him, my lord, that your Highness
could not see him ; but he said, that even if the
Regent were in bed, he must see him ; and he
won't go away."

"Admit him."

The servant left the room.

" When will this weary day close ? It has been
the longest day of my life, and the dreariest."

Herr Litmann was the great Jew banker of the Court. His interests were closely allied with those of the Regent; and in his hands vast sums had been deposited by the Duke. Before dinner Herr Litmann had been closeted with the Regent, and had informed him that there was a plot against his government, and even against his life. The Archbishop of Novogorod had preceded Litmann earlier in the day; and he, too, had come to give the Regent information of the conspiracy.

Herr Litmann entered. He was evidently in a state of great agitation. Being a stout unwieldy man, and having hurried up the stairs, he was almost breathless, and gasped out his first sentences.

"It's all true. There's not a moment to be lost. I'm certain of it. He was with the Duchess again in the forenoon — disguised. Why disguised? You don't know that man. That fool, too, her husband, has been talking again, most insolently, of your Highness. The people murmur in the streets."

"That is no new thing, my good Litmann. This excellent people always have murmured in the streets, ever since I have known them. Why man, the Empress is not yet buried; and all the thought, if thought it can be called, which the Grand Duchess can command, is given to that ceremonial, and to her place in it. The day after to-morrow, Münnich goes to the frontier. It is all settled. I have provided for it. I take at least as much care for my life, Litmann, as you for your roubles."

"By the god of my fathers, your care will be too late."

The Regent drew himself up haughtily, and said, "Herr Litmann, you are a shrewd man, and money grows in your hands; but I am not aware that you have had much to do with the government of human beings, unless it be your own clerks. Allow me to do my work, and to know how it should be done."

The astute Jew perceived that any further effort on his part was hopeless. He said not another word, but rushed from the room ab-

ruptly, without even a parting salutation. The
Duke was, in his eyes, a doomed man, whom it
was scarcely worth while to consider any more.
Herr Litmann spent the remainder of that night
in concealing what jewels and specie he thought
he could venture to hide away, while still leaving
large portions of his wealth unconcealed. He
was almost minded to seek safety in flight; but,
as there was a considerable amount of his property which he could not carry with him, the
chain between that property and him was too
strong to be broken at a moment's notice.

The Regent was again left alone. "Jews,
gypsies, archbishops — all of them have their
special avenues of information. Rascality
reaches them by separate roads. What they
say, is true. I needed not their information;
I saw the danger myself; but it is a long way
from the frontier to St. Petersburg. Münnich
may scheme there. That Scotchman, Keith, may
scheme elsewhere: there are other generals who
are mine. I am not a Cromwell to go to bed in
armour, change my room from night to night,

and try to deceive my own guards as to my whereabouts. I may be a tyrant. I don't dislike that boy for telling me so; but at least, I am not a coward."*

The Regent remained for some time buried in thought, and then retired to his chamber.

---

* It appears that the stories about Cromwell, much exaggerated, were still rife on the Continent; and the Regent's conduct, on this occasion, was contrasted with that of Cromwell.

BOOK I.

—◆—

CHAPTER IX.

RESULT OF THE CONSPIRACY.

Ivan had spoken to his master of the lateness of the hour; but it was not what we should call late, seeing that it was but eleven o'clock when the last of the Regent's guests departed. This, however, was a very late hour at a period when great feasts were held at two o'clock in the day.

The Field Marshal, well aware that the Regent's spies were everywhere, and that some of them were, perhaps, members of his own household, drove home to his palace, and went at

once to bed. But little sleep, as he afterwards
said, had he that night. Indeed there is as little
hope of sleep for the framers of a conspiracy, on
the eve of its outbreak, as for affianced brides the
night before their marriage.

At two o'clock in the morning Münnich rose,
and sent for his aid-de-camp, Colonel Manstein,
whom he had apprised that he should want his
services very early in the morning. It may be
conjectured that Marshal Münnich had not made
up his mind, before he went to bed, at what time
he should commence his enterprise, otherwise he
would have told Manstein that he should want
him in the middle of the night. Probably, as
Münnich lay tossing on his bed in anxious
thought, each moment's delay in the commence-
ment of that enterprise seemed doubly hazardous
to him. An additional reason for supposing
that he had not finally decided upon the exact
time of action, may be deduced from the fact
that he had made no arrangement for a further
interview with the Grand Duchess. Probably
that pregnant question asked by the Regent,

and his manner of asking it, decided any doubts that still remained in the Field Marshal's mind.

The enterprise, indeed, if undertaken at this moment, was certainly most hazardous. To make his way by night into the Winter Palace, where the Grand Duchess dwelt, was alone a matter of great difficulty, and he did not dare to take the final step without her acquiescence, however wrung from her. The state of insecurity at that time was such, that the palaces of the grandees of Russia were most strictly guarded; and both at the Winter Palace and the Summer Palace, there were not only sentinels at every entrance, but there were piquets, consisting of forty men, posted in front of these palaces. If but one of these guards were to do his duty and to give the alarm, the attempt would be frustrated; and failure in such an enterprise was certain death for the conspirators.

Manstein came, and the Field Marshal drove with him in a coach to the Winter Palace.

Their forethought in having arranged that the regiment on duty should be one devoted to them, and of which indeed the Field Marshal was Colonel, was most serviceable. They were allowed to pass, rather to the private disgust of the severe disciplinarian, Manstein. The Field Marshal knew his way about the palace, and he made at once for the bed-room of the Grand Duke and Duchess. In the ante-chamber the favourite, Juliana de Mengden, was sleeping. Münnich awoke her; and, after some parley, persuaded her to awake the royal pair, who were sleeping in the next room. It was the Grand Duchess alone who came out to see him. We may reasonably conjecture, for it was never known, that the Grand Duke did not partake the views and wishes of his wife, and at any rate wished to keep himself free from responsibility. Strange to say, the irresolution of the Duchess seemed to have vanished. Their conference was but brief; and, at the end of it, the Marshal ordered Manstein to summon all the officers who were on guard at the Palace.

Her Highness made a short speech to the assembled officers, recounting the injuries which the Imperial family had suffered from the Regent; declaring that it was impossible for her any longer to endure his conduct; and stating, that she was determined to have him apprehended. To Marshal Münnich she had committed the duty of seizing the person of the Regent; and she trusted that these officers would implicitly obey the Marshal's orders. They made no difficulty whatever as regards obeying the Grand Duchess's commands. Whereupon she gave them her hand to kiss, and they went downstairs with the Marshal, who got the guard under arms.

The men were ordered to load their muskets. An officer, with some of the rank and file, was left on guard with the colours. The remainder of the men went with Münnich to the Summer Palace. This body halted at a short distance from the building. Then the Marshal sent Manstein alone to the piquet which was stationed in front of the Palace. Manstein told them the whole story, and that the Field Marshal had received the Grand Duchess's orders to seize the Regent.

In this vast Empire it is probable that the Regent had no real friend. The officers and men of this piquet—his own guard—made no more objection to the proposal than the Grand Duchess's men had made. In short, they said that they were ready to give their assistance, if it was necessary, in seizing the Regent.

Manstein returned to the Field Marshal with these good tidings. He was then ordered to put himself with an officer at the head of twenty men, to enter the Palace, and capture the Regent; and, in case he made any resistance, to put him to death.

Manstein entered the Palace alone, leaving the soldiers at the entrance. The sentinels allowed him to pass in without any address on his part to them, for they fancied that he had come, as a friend to the Regent, upon some matter of urgent importance. But after he had entered the palace, he was extremely embarrassed as to which way to take. Soon he came upon some servants, who were waiting in an ante-chamber; but, being desirous of avoiding all suspicion, he walked on as if he knew the way to the Regent's room. After he had passed through this ante-chamber, he went through two other rooms which were vacant. Then he came to some folding-doors. These were locked, but fortunately for him, the servants had neglected to fasten them by sliding the bolts at the top and the bottom, so that he easily forced the doors open.

Upon what minute circumstances do the greatest events depend! For, if the Regent had escaped, the fear of men would have furnished him with a party to uphold his legal right; and, at the least, a great civil war might have been the result of this conspiracy.

When Manstein had forced these doors, he found that he had entered the chamber where the Regent and his wife were lying. Biron's sleep, after that day of fearful anxiety, was so profound that not even the noise which Manstein had made in forcing open the doors had awakened him. His wife, too, slept soundly. Manstein undrew the curtain, and desired to speak with the Regent. Thereupon, both husband and wife started up in surprize, and began to clamour for assistance, "judging rightly enough that this intruder had not come to bring them any good news."* The Regent sprang from the bed. Manstein threw himself upon him, and held him tightly until the guards came in. It is evident that some of the soldiers must have followed upon Manstein's steps. The Regent, a powerful man, dealt Manstein and the soldiers some hard blows with his fist. They struck at him with the butt-ends of their muskets. At length, throwing him down on the floor, they gagged him with a handkerchief, bound his hands with an officer's sash, took him to the guard-room, where they covered him with a soldier's cloak, and then conveyed him in the Marshal's coach as a prisoner to the Winter Palace.

* Manstein's ' Memoirs of Russia.'

While the soldiers were struggling with the Regent, his Duchess had got out of bed and had followed him into the street, when a soldier took her in his arms, and asked Manstein what he should do with her. He bade him carry her back to her chamber; but the soldier not caring, it seems, to take this trouble, threw her down on the ground in the midst of the snow, and there left her. The captain of the guard, finding her in this piteous condition, had some clothes brought to her, and re-conducted her to the apartment she had occupied.

The Regent's brother and other of his relatives and adherents were also seized that night.

The Regent was not allowed shelter in the Winter Palace. Miserably clad as he was, and exposed to the snow which was then falling, he was kept standing at the door, where he was subjected to the insults of the people, for it was now morning. At last, some hours afterwards, he and his Duchess were put into an open carriage to be conveyed to Schlüsselberg, a

journey of about thirty miles. There was, moreover, a fearful addition to his sufferings. Companions were provided for him on that journey,
the very sight of whom must have caused anguish
to his soul. Hastily there were collected from
the prisons about thirty State prisoners, all of
whom could reproach him for their imprisonment.
Nor did they fail to do so. Some of them must
have been with him in one of the large and lum-
bering coaches or waggons which were provided
for the conveyance of prisoners. Andrew Ja-
cowitz, State Councillor and Cabinet Secretary,
lately condemned by the Regent, was now one of
his companions in misery. This poor man had been
so severely knouted that he was injured for life.

In this sorry fashion, and with such friends and
companions, did the delicately-nurtured Regent
pursue his weary way to that fortress to which
his signature had sent so many other wretched
beings, and which he could not reach before midnight.

Ivan de Biron was also one of this mournful
cavalcade; and, as the Regent's private secretary,

had to listen to the reproaches and curses which
were heaped upon him, being naturally supposed
to be nearly as guilty as his master.

The feelings of the Grand Duchess during the
three or four hours that elapsed between the time
of her speech to the officers, and the return of
Münnich with his prisoner, must have been very
grievous and anxious. The slightest noise in the
streets made her heart beat with fear. It might
announce, not the return of Münnich, but the
approach of the revengeful Biron, who, after
the failure of such an enterprise, would no longer
hesitate to lay violent hands not only upon her
Imperial self, but upon her darling child and her
beloved favourite. She must have known full
well, that by consenting to Münnich's scheme,
she had risked the reign, if not the life, of a
child who might hereafter justly reproach his
mother for placing all their fortunes in such
hazard.

On the following morning, all the regiments
that were at St. Petersburg were ordered to
assemble around the palace. The Grand Duchess

then declared herself Regent of the Empire
during the minority of the Emperor. She, at
the same time, put on the Collar of the Order
of St. Andrew; and every one took a new oath of
fidelity, in which the Grand Duchess was mentioned by name, as had not been done in that
imposed by the Regent. There were none that
did not make great demonstrations of joy at
seeing themselves delivered from the severity
of Biron. From that moment everything was
quiet. Even the piquets were taken away, which
the Duke of Courland had posted in the streets,
to prevent commotions during his regency. And
yet there were some shrewd persons, who, though
rejoicing at this great event, prognosticated that
it would not be the last of its kind; and that those
who had been the most active in bringing it
about, would be the first that would be the
victims of another revolution.

After an examination of the prisoners, which,
in the Duke of Courland's case, took place at the
fortress of Schlüsselberg, he and his adherents
were banished to Siberia. Among them was

General Bismarck, a brother-in-law of the Regent.

The obsequies of the defunct Empress were then celebrated with great pomp. It is remarkable that these occurrences should have taken place in the short time that elapsed between the death of the Empress and her funeral. So soon was it that her prophecy of evil for her favourite, on his assumption of the regency, was to be fulfilled.

The conspiracy, of which the issue has just been narrated, was of so remarkable a character that it deserves to have a few comments made upon it.

The course of conspiracies is wont to be singularly uniform. The previous transactions mostly occupy much time; and day by day, or at least, week by week, some new person is introduced into the plot. The aids and appliances thought to be necessary, tend to become far too elaborate, each new appliance brings in a fresh element for possible detection. Happily, too, for mankind, their habitual faithlessness

serves them in this instance. Eventually there
is nearly sure to be some person, who, actuated
by fear, by the hope of favour, or by pity,
becomes the traitor, and either directly, or by
some pregnant hint, betrays the plot. So it
happens that a very small percentage of projects
of this kind succeeds.

Never was there a conspiracy so swiftly formed,
so swiftly matured, so swiftly betrayed, and so
swiftly executed, as this conspiracy against the
powerful Duke of Courland.

The state of Russian society is also indicated,
by the remarkable manner in which a knowledge
of the plot must have spread through the
capital.

In an incredibly short time, a conspiracy
known at first to the Field Marshal only and a
few important personages, is so widely bruited
about, that Christian prelates (for other great
dignitaries of the Church, besides the Archbishop
of Novogorod, had called upon the Regent and
had given him information), and also the Jew
banker Litmann, were, it appears, thoroughly

versed in what was going on. That it was to be
an undertaking by night, and that the Regent
had divined this, is almost certain from the
alarming question which he put to the Field
Marshal in the presence of Manstein and others
who have recorded this most interesting circumstance.

The Regent, throughout these proceedings,
is little to be blamed. With his vast knowledge
of conspiracies, even if he believed in the
existence of this one, it was but in accordance
with his experience, that it should take time to
come to maturity; and he never imagined that
any overt act would take place before the ceremonies of the late Empress's funeral should have
been solemnized. The character of Count
Münnich, imperfectly read by the Regent, did
not allow him to believe that this gay, talkative,
restless, brilliant man, could act with the speed
and force of a dark-souled and determined conspirator.

The Grand Vizier, when the news was brought
to Constantinople of the downfall of the Regent,

made the following remark, "So then this Russian Regent has met with a still harder fate than has fallen to the lot of scarcely any of my predecessors." It seems as if the Grand Vizier abhorred exile more than death.

Ovid tells us, meaning to show forth the full misery of exile, how his feet, sympathizing with his soul, almost refused to quit the threshold.

> Ter limen tetigi ; ter sum revocatus : et ipse,
> Indulgens animo, pes mihi tardus erat.

No lingering of this kind was allowed to the unhappy Regent of Russia. He went to sleep, a Sovereign Prince, and an all-powerful prime minister : he awoke, to find himself at once, as may be said, a prisoner and an exile.

BOOK II.

BOOK II.

—◆—

CHAPTER I.

On the fall of the Regent there were doubtless many persons in St. Petersburg who, in their rude way, felt and thought what one of the greatest of Latin poets has expressed in a passage almost unrivalled for force and beauty.

A certain Rufinus was the prime minister of the Emperor Theodosius, and was as hateful to the Roman people as the Duke of Courland had been to the Russian people—and far more justly hateful.

The poet Claudian says that his dubious mind

had often been drawn this way and that, thinking whether the gods cared for mankind, whether there was any ruler of the world, or whether mortal affairs flowed on with undirected course. When he beheld the strictness and the beauty of the laws of nature—the sea contained within its prescribed bounds—the invariable recurrence of the seasons, the succession of night to day—then he thought that all things were governed by the counsels of God. On the other hand, when he looked at human affairs involved in such darkness, the wicked flourishing, the pious tormented, then his religion glided away from him. He thought the world was ruled by chance, not by design; that there were either no deities, or that they took no heed of mortal men. At length, Rufinus fell. His fate appeased this tumult of contending thoughts in the poet's mind, and absolved the gods.

> Abstulit hunc tandem Rufini pœna tumultum.
> Absolvitque Deos.

There must have been those in Russia who felt that their hard thoughts of Providence were

now removed, now that the tyrant Biron had
been hurled from power. The state of siege in
which the city had been kept was set aside; the
spies were dumbfounded for the moment; the
people breathed again.

The course of this narrative does not allow the
reader to follow in detail the events which took
place in the capital on the deposition of the
Regent. The scene is at once changed to a
distant region.

The time was evening; the place was a small
town in Siberia, named Pelem; and the season of
the year was spring. The word town, however,
is a very dignified name to give to the miserable
wooden hovels which were clustered together at
small distances from each other.

It must not be supposed that Siberia is a
country wholly devoid of great natural beauty
and of great natural fertility. Indeed, there are
parts of Siberia which rival, if not excel, the
grandest scenery in Switzerland. But at this

season of the year, and in this region, the land-
scape had a most depressing appearance.

Almost everywhere throughout the world that
season is odious, with its sunshine like the smile
of a false man, and its bright bitterness far more
intolerable than the downright gloom of honest
old November. But, in Siberia, the treacherous
time of spring presents its worst and most re-
pulsive aspect.

The snow had begun to melt, and tufts of
scanty herbage were here and there beginning to
make their appearance. In the far distance there
were snowy mountains still retaining all their
beauty. These, however, were scarcely visible, for
a thick dark mist was creeping up, and partially
obscured them. In and around the town the
snow was trodden down; and all nature had that
aspect of a transition state which in such regions
is most deplorable and most depressing.

Two buildings alone in this town stood out as
superior to the rest. One was the church, the
colour of which would have attracted the notice
of any person on first entering the town, as it

presented an appearance so different from the dim tints which the surrounding wooden houses had acquired. Outside it was whitewashed, and gaudily ornamented with various devices in blue and red colouring. Its roof was of some metallic substance, which glittered in midday; and which, even now, shone meteor-like above the mist. It was lighted up, and was prepared for evening service.

The other building, though constructed of wood like the rest of the dwellings, was of two stories, and was surrounded by palisades. No light was visible in it, for the windows were so designed as to look into a small courtyard at the rear of the house. Two persons, already known in this story, inhabited that building. One of them was a young man of frank and engaging manners, who was on friendly terms with all the other exiles; the other was a man of mature age, who, though he had been for some months a resident in that town, had never been seen in daylight, face to face, by any of its inhabitants. Sometimes he had been seen at midnight walking on the flat roof of this house; and, if it were a darker evening

than usual when the cattle came back to the
town, he would then, closely muffled, make his
appearance on the roof. This seemed to be his
only pleasure, as it was to another remarkable
person, who, at a future period, occupied the
same house, of which circumstance there is a
tradition that has come down to the present
day.

The present occupants of the house were Ernest
de Biron, Duke of Courland, the late Regent of
Russia, and his secretary, Ivan de Biron.

At the northern end of the town, and almost
in its precincts, was a large forest. At the time
described, a young girl, in peasant dress, had
brought her burthen of felled wood to the
extremity of the forest near the town. There
was no one in that small community to whom
the pleasant sights and sounds which belong to
a forest were more soothing and more acceptable
than to that maiden.

In all climes a forest is perhaps the most
beautiful, and at any rate the most gracious pro-

duct of nature, but in Siberia it has an especial pre-eminence; and, very significantly, the inhabitants of that dreary region have adopted the tree as a sacred symbol.

Each of the senses, sound, sight, and smell, must be delighted by the gratification it receives in a Siberian forest. Variety of colours, infinite play of light and shade, diversity of odours—not omitting the rich, wholesome odour of the pine, and that low murmuring noise which prevents solitude, yet scarcely hinders silence—are all to be met with there.

Then, too, there is something to be seen which aptly reminds one of human life. In the forest the individual tree, as in the crowded city the individual human being, is often dwarfed, stunted, and controlled in its existence by its immediate neighbours; but yet it inclines forward and pushes forth its branches towards every inlet of air and light that it can possibly attain to. This gives that variety of form which is so delightful to the lover of nature. There is the tree which, from the near oppression of its neighbour, becomes only a polished column with a growth of wood and foliage at the head, while there is another of a different species which throws out its vigour in its lower branches, and is only poor and barren at the summit. Then, again, there is the absence of that result of contending elements, the wind—a creature that greatly disturbs human dignity and prevents meditation, except with the healthiest and hardiest of human beings.

It was no wonder that the maiden should have chosen the forest of Pelem as her favourite resort. But there were causes, independently of the attractions described above, which made that forest most welcome to her.

This young girl had travelled with her father; had seen the old towns of Belgium, France, and Italy; and had imbibed that love for whatever is ancient, which is often strongest in those whose country affords the fewest relics of the past. Old trees were about the oldest things that could be seen in such a new country as Siberia; and, on that account alone, this wood was very dear to the girl, and much frequented by her.

She sat down upon a fallen tree which lay nearly across the pathway to the town. It adjoined one of the finest trees in the forest; and, at the point of junction, parasitic plants and mosses had grown up abundantly, forming a nook which made a pleasant seat for two persons. Hence it was that this fallen tree had not been used as firewood, though it was so near the town, and had, indeed gained a significant Russian name, which, being translated, means "For him and her."

She was feeling very glad that the hardest part of her day's work was ended. She sat quietly for some time, so quietly that the squirrels and other small denizens of the wood came out from their hiding-places, and ran hither and thither, regardless of her presence. She seemed to be listening intently, as for the approach of some one who would make more noise amongst the brushwood by his coming than the little creatures which played around her. Then there was heard in the distance the lowing of cattle returning from their scanty pasturage to their stalls in the town. Each one of the herd had a bell round its neck; and a

merry sound of jangling music was borne upon
the breeze. This sound seemed to delight the
girl, for she sprang up joyfully, and exclaimed,
" He will come now. I shall ever love the music of
these bells." And then again she sat down upon
the tree, and assumed a look of perfect composure
and indifference.

The musical approach of the cattle had been
heard a few minutes earlier in the town than in
the forest ; and no sooner was it heard, than Ivan
de Biron had gone out from the house before
described, and had walked, apparently without
any purpose, to the forest. He seemed though
to know whither to direct his steps, for he soon
approached the spot where the girl was sitting,
and sat down by her side.

They were a comely pair to look upon. The
maiden was beautiful with the beauty of radiant
health and strength. The attempt to describe
man or woman fully by words, is to ask more
from language than it can perform. Nevertheless the attempt must sometimes be made.

The face of this maiden was a most remarkable

one.   In looking at her, you felt assured that the
family from which she sprung must have been of
Tartar origin; but all the peculiarities of form
and feature belonging to that race, were
tempered into beauty.   The eyes were somewhat
obliquely set in the face; but the colour of them
was not that which belongs to the Tartar race,
but was of a soft blue.   The eye-brows and eye-
lashes were dark, and the former had no curve of
beauty, but were perfectly straight.   The nose
was slightly *retroussé*.   The mouth was larger
and wider than is generally supposed to be con-
sistent with beauty.   The general colour of the
countenance, upon which so much indication of
character depends, must originally have been pale,
but it was now bronzed, and even reddened by
constant exposure to the severe climate.   The
hands were encased in fur gloves; but, hardened
as they were by toil, no one who had seen them
would have supposed that they were the hands
of the young and beautiful Princess Marie
Andréevna Serbatoff, who, a winter or two ago,
had been held in St. Petersburg and Moscow, to

be one of the most beautiful young women of her time.

The expression of her countenance was very variable. Sometimes it was tender and submissive; at others it was capable of expressing the fiercest indignation, and did express it.

The young man and the maiden did not sit together, talking idly; but they divided between them the work that had to be done of chopping up the larger pieces of fire-wood, which were afterwards to be carried to her father's hut. There was even a playful contention between them as to who should take the harder work.

"Ah! Marie," exclaimed the young man, "this is not the proper work for you."

"I do not desire to be pitied, Ivan. You may think ill of me, but I do not know whether, if I were to speak truly, I should not say that this was a pleasanter life than that which I led with my French and German governesses. And then one sleeps at nights—such sleep as I never slept in any of my father's palaces. But oh! my father ! If he could but endure this life, I should be content. His wretchedness wearies us, and bears us to the ground."

" And so you do not miss all the sweet flatteries that must so often have been addressed to the Princess Marie ? "

" Miss them ! I loathed them. You young men all talk the same talk, Ivan ; but it is poor stuff at the best. If the old wore masks, it is they whom we should love, for they can say something to us which approaches to sense. Some few of them, at least, can talk, whereas you boys can only prattle."

" Nay, Marie, but you cannot say this of me, for, in the times of your splendour, I did not dare to talk to you. I only looked from a distance at the beautiful young princess, unapproachable by a poor private secretary, though he were—"

" Though he were ? Pray finish the sentence Ivan, and disclose the mystery which surrounds you. Who is the other who lives with you ? "

" An exile like the rest of us."

"Exiled by that detestable wretch, the Duke of Courland?"

"Well,—yes—he was the cause of our exile —an exile, for my part, which I cannot but bless, as it has brought me near to thee, my dearest Marie."

"You are somewhat familiar, sir; I am no one's 'dearest Marie,' but my father's. Are you noble!"

"And if I were not, would that make so much difference, Marie? I should have thought the life we lead might have effaced these artificial differences of station."

"And so they should. We, almost serfs and certain beggars, may well dispense with all the mockery of titles. But I would you had been noble, Ivan. It would make us more akin. Poor youth! and so you, too, are one of the thousands of victims of this barbarous man, this Biron. And in what conspiracy did this smooth face partake? It must have been a deep one. It must have taxed the vigilance of the great Duke himself, and all his spies, to have unravelled a plot devised in such a head as this."

And here, with somewhat of fondness, partially disguised by mockery, she placed her hand upon the head of the young man, and looked laughingly into his eyes. For his part, he was half amused, half offended, by her ridicule. For, as amongst real criminals, transcendent crime has always a certain dignity and respect attending it, and great criminals are wont to despise petty offenders, so, in Siberia, where past treasons were the common talk, those were the great men, the aristocrats in this miserable population, whose conspiracies against the favourite had been of the largest character, and the most nearly approaching to success.

At this moment there resounded through the still air a hymn, which was being chanted in the little church. It was a hymn well known both to the youth and the maiden, which, indeed, they had often sung side by side, and which spoke of mercy and forgiveness, and of all men being brethren.

They listened for some minutes to these sweet sounds, and sweet they were, for no people in the world, perhaps, not even the Italians, have so passionate a love for music, and so much skill in singing a certain melancholy music of their own, as the Russian peasantry.   And here, in that small wooden church, were not merely peasant voices to be heard, but the more refined voices of many an exiled noble.

The hymn did not succeed in soothing the fierce spirit of the maiden.   On the contrary, the gracious words did but excite her indignation. "'Mercy! Forgiveness! All men brethren!' These priests, and those who think with them, may chant these unreal mockeries; but who can forgive such injuries as I have suffered? My little sister died upon the road; and the barbarians who drove us onward, would not even stay to let us see her buried. My mother's misery caused her blindness; and my father, once his sovereign's favourite, and as true a councillor as ever breathed, is now a moody man, half crazed by sorrow, who paces all day long our narrow room, muttering curses on his persecutor. And they shall be fulfilled; these curses. Would that I had the man before me now! with this hatchet I would hew him down myself. Look not so scared, my gentle Ivan. I hate him all the more for your sake. Your conspiracy must have been a fine plot indeed! Why one man can always kill one man, if he is only brave enough to put his own life in peril. Had you so ventured—Oh, but I would not have had you do so!—that wretch, the Duke of Courland, would not be living now."

During this outbreak of passion, Ivan had not said a word to interrupt his much-loved Marie. But there was a something in his look which showed displeasure, almost disgust. Her ready apprehension did not fail to see it. With the swift impetuosity of her character, she changed her mood; looked beseechingly at him, and no longer like the tigress, but like the mild and gentle fawn.

" You do not love me now, Ivan? I will be gentle: yes, very gentle. But I may at least, hate him, our common enemy, may I not ?—the cause of all our miseries, that Duke of Courland."

Ivan made no answer. The girl sought to take his hand, which he gave somewhat reluctantly, but which she fondly pressed. After a few minutes' silence, she exclaimed, " I must go, my father waits for me. I am his only comfort, Ivan ; and I am ashamed that I waste with you moments which should all be given to him."

So saying, she sprang up lightly ; collected together the wood which they had prepared for firewood ; and went hastily towards her father's log hut. The young man did not accompany her ; but, after remaining a short time in the forest, returned to his home ; and his looks were very downcast as he entered it.

We all have different ambitions. The one which occupied this young man's soul was of an unusual kind. He had often thought to himself, what he would most desire in the world, and had come to the conclusion that it was—to be supremely loved. That seemed to him the best and greatest success in life. This girl, he felt, did love him greatly ; perhaps as much as it was in her nature to love any one ; but was it of that overpowering kind which would conquer a disposition so foreign and so unpleasing to his own ?

BOOK II.

CHAPTER II.

It was at a late hour on that same day, that the door of that same house which Ivan had entered, was again opened; and the Duke of Courland, with a cloak wrapped round him, concealing his countenance, stepped out and walked away from the town. The scene was now very beautiful. It was a bright night. The moon and the stars shone with a radiance only to be seen in those latitudes. The mist had disappeared, and the peaks of the snowy mountains were now visible.

Miserable as were most of the elder inhabi-

tants of that town, this man's misery exceeded
theirs. He spoke; and his was no tame soli-
loquy, but was loudly uttered, as if he were
addressing a multitude.

"The basest of created creatures," he exclaimed, "are men! Why, even their ghosts
adore prosperity. They did not haunt me when
I was all-powerful; but now they are always
with me, mocking and gibbering, and shouting
'murder.' I fled from them in the house, and
here they are now in multitudes.

"Why did you thwart me? why cross my
path, I say? It was death to cross it, and you
should have known that. Away with you, fools!
The State demanded it; and I, the Duke of
Courland, was the State. Do not crowd about
me so."

Such were the moody, almost mad utterances
of this unhappy man, who for hours would
address these imaginary followers with mingled
scorn and threats.

If, however, he did not fear these impalpable
spectres, conjured up by his remorse, he feared

the living victims of his cruelty ; for, on the first approach of day-light, he walked swiftly back to that dwelling which he had never suffered any stranger to enter, and from which he never emerged except at midnight.

BOOK II.

——◆——

CHAPTER III.

RECALL OF IVAN FROM SIBERIA.

FROM the conversation, which has been recounted, between the Princess Marie Andréevna Serbatoff and her lover, Ivan de Biron, a very wrong idea might be formed of that young man's character and disposition. He was one of those frank, kindly, good-natured persons whose real strength of character is often concealed by these amiable qualities of kindness and good-nature. He was quite unfitted to cope with the Princess in an encounter of wit. She affected to treat him as if he were a mere

boy, much younger than herself; but, in reality,
she had the greatest respect, as well as love for
him, and was even a little afraid of him. The
calmness of his nature often made her ashamed
of her own vehemence and versatility; though,
at the same time, it provoked her to a frequent
display of these very qualities. Vehemence
and versatility are mostly signs of weakness;
and in this respect, the Princess, though anything but a weak person, sometimes presented
an unfavourable contrast to the firm and strong
character of her lover.

Her life had been supremely wretched until
Ivan had come amongst them. Her mother's
blindness, her father's irritable despondency,
the death of her sister, had all been causes
which created deep depression of spirits, sufficient to subdue even this brilliant and lively
girl. She had jestingly pretended that her
present mode of life was endurable when compared with her former life, passed with severe
governesses and tutors at St. Petersburg or
Moscow. But, until Ivan came, she had

mourned, not only for her parents, but for herself, when she recalled to mind the brilliant scenes upon which she had just begun to enter, and where she had been welcomed with all the courteous flattery that was sure to be addressed ·to the beautiful daughter of a great house, the head of which was in high favour with the late Empress Anne, until that favour had attracted the jealous notice of the supreme favourite, the Duke of Courland.

The household tasks, which were obliged to be performed even by the most delicate young women in this dreary place of exile, were, at first, no slight burden, and no slight suffering. But, as it has often been seen in similar cases, and as may be seen in the present day in our Colonies, these delicate women are wont to meet that part of their fate with a power of resolve, and with an equanimity, which surprises themselves and all who see them. It is even probable that these domestic duties and labours prove the greatest source of comfort to those who fulfill them.

The most miserable among the exiles were
those who, like the Princess's father and mother,
were chiefly employed in bringing before their
own minds the recollections of a brilliant past,
and imbittering their nature by a constant
expression of hatred to those who had caused·
their exile.   Hatred is very catching ; and it
would almost have been contrary to nature for
the Princess Marie, even had she not been somewhat of a fierce disposition herself, not to have
imbibed some of the unbounded hatred which
her father felt, and hour by hour, expressed,
for his persecutor, the Duke of Courland.

It was but little in the way of political news
that ever reached these exiles.   They did not
know that the Empress Anne was dead; and
the Prince supposed that his great enemy was
still supreme at the Russian Court, and was still
sending fresh batches of exiles to the remote
parts of Siberia.   The escort which had brought
the ex-regent to this town of Pelem, had arrived
in the evening, and had left on the ensuing
morning.   It may be doubted whether the

rough soldiers who had formed the Duke of
Courland's escort, and who had received their
prisoner at a stage one hundred versts from
Pelem, their ultimate destination, were aware
of the rank of that prisoner, or, if they had
been aware, would have been in the least
degree interested by it. They performed their
hard duty in their hard way, and troubled themselves very little about political events.

Whatever may have been the cause, it is certain that the exiles in this town had not the
slightest notion that the moody man who dwelt
in this two-storied house, and who had only been
seen in the distance by one or two of them at
early dawn, was their enemy and persecutor;
the man to whom most of them owed their
present state of suffering and exile.

An event, however, now occurred, which
would be likely to defeat all the Duke of Courland's hopes of being able to remain unknown
to his companions.

At first, every one, however remotely connected with the banished Duke, had been seized

and sentenced to a Siberian exile. Count
Münnich was not a man who was disposed to
do his business by halves. The ex-regent's long
tenure of power had introduced his friends, or
those who were supposed to be such, into every
department of the State; and Count Münnich
was naturally afraid of any counter-revolution
that might be attempted by a number of disappointed and desperate men, who would be
aware that under the new *régime* they would be
looked upon with but little favour. They were
accordingly dealt with in the severe manner
that partisans of a defeated faction were sure
to be dealt with, in such a country and at such
a time.

The general joy, however, which was manifested by the great body of the people, at the
downfall of the Regent, tended to reassure both
Count Münnich and the new Duchess Regent.
It was doubtless soon discovered, that in Biron's
family and household, there were many who
would have regarded his downfall with delight,
if it had not involved themselves in ruin.

It now appeared, for men dared to speak out openly, that our young hero, Ivan, had, on more than one occasion, sought to mitigate his master's fury ; and had even dared, secretly, to give orders in that master's name, that certain exiles should be humanely treated by the escort that conveyed them on the outset of their journey from St. Petersburg or Moscow. The pleasant and comely countenance of the youth had been noticed by the Duchess Regent, to whom, on some occasion during the first few days of his regency, the Duke of Courland had sent him to obtain a signature, or to arrange some other small matter of business.

It was not known at the time, and Ivan himself never knew who it was, that interceded in his favour with the Duchess Regent, or with Count Münnich, all-powerful for the time. But the intercession was successful; and an order was despatched to the place of the Duke of Courland's banishment, recalling his private secretary, Ivan, and one or two other persons of inferior note, who had been exiled to that town

at the earlier time of Prince Menschikoff's downfall.

The persons who brought this order did not
return as quickly as the Duke of Courland's
escort had done. One of them was a civilian,
the secretary to the Governor of one of the provinces of Siberia. This man was cognizant of all
that had occurred at Court; and he had not
been many hours in the town before it was
known to all the inhabitants that the late Empress Anne was dead; that the Duke of Courland had been Regent for a few days; that he
was deposed from power, and was now an exile
like themselves. The secretary to the Governor
was, of course, aware that Biron himself was
there. He had gone first to the ex-regent's
house, with the order of release for Ivan; but
he had been moved by the Duke's prayers and
entreaties—so far as not to betray the fact of the
presence there of the late Sovereign' minister.
The wary official probably bethought himself
that, in the frequent revolutions to which
Russia was subject, there might come one

which would bring Biron back to power
again; and the Duke, he well knew, was
not a man who would ever forget an injury.
This official person, therefore, promised his
Highness to be silent as to the Duke's whereabouts; and he kept his word.

BOOK II.

———◆———

CHAPTER IV.

IVAN'S PREPARATIONS FOR DEPARTURE.

PRINCE SERBATOFF was in an ecstacy of delight when he heard of the discomfiture of his great enemy. "It makes me young again," he exclaimed. "Think of the joy of thousands, who must know now, or I trust they do, that this villain is suffering what he has so long made all of us suffer. How is it, Marie, that you do not partake our joy? Even your mother no longer weeps. Look out now. It is a scene of delight. Behold the mists crawling up from this hideous surface of the earth. Ha! it is cold.

Would that it were ten times colder! I hate the spring now. Why does it come so early? He should have had all the agonies of a Siberian winter, to burst upon him in the first moments of his exile, as I had. There are no supreme joys, Marie, without some drawback: and you, girl, I do not understand you. Dance, sing, be merry, put wood upon the fire. We will use it all up to-day; and, sitting round its merry blaze, will think of him, and hope, for God is good, that there is no one to serve him, none of his slaves with him, no one to tend his fire. And his hands were delicate. The soft hands of a girl—the hands that were thought so beautiful by his vain and empty-headed mistress."

The Princess Marie listened with a dejected countenance to these wild ravings of her father. Leaving the room upon some pretext of domestic work, she thus spoke to herself, as, with hasty steps, she walked up and down in front of their hut :—

" How base am I! I should rejoice at Ivan's happiness, but, oh, what misery to me! Would that he had never come—that I had never been mocked by the joy of his companionship! And then to lose him—lose him for ever; for some girl will treat him better than I have done with my caprice and folly. And men are not as constant as we are. And then he is so loveable and loving. He has not come near me. He fears to come near me. He fears to show how happy he is in quitting this detested place. But there will be protestations and promises, and vows. I distrust them all. He does not come, and to whom should he have been the first to tell his good fortune? Who would have sympathised with him most deeply? For I will do so, whatever it shall cost me. We are not as the meaner women, unable to command our feelings; or, at least, we have the power to conceal them."

She had been looking down upon the ground, as she had uttered these words to herself; and, looking up, she saw that Ivan was approaching her.

No joy sat upon his countenance, but instead of that, the utmost dejection.

"You have heard the news, Marie," he said in a low voice; and, as he spoke, he put his arm round her. She, however, disengaged herself from it, and said, in calm tones : " Yes, I have heard it, Ivan, and it is glorious news indeed. Recalled to St. Petersburg, perhaps to Court favour, you will become a great man, Ivan. You must quite forget us poor exiles who remain ; but how," she added with a smile, " shall I ever find another fellow-woodsman with his kind aid to make my labour light ?   To-day we were to have sung together in the church, and I was to have practised with you and taught you. 'Tis little I can teach, but I am the better musician.   Say, shall we try it ? for I suppose you do not leave us suddenly, and we will have a hymn of joy for your departure."

The only answer that he made, was to take both her hands in his, and, looking at her stead-fastly, if not severely, he uttered her name, ' Marie ' reproachfully.

She again disengaged herself from him, and began talking much in the same strain in which she had soliloquised, all of which talk went to show that she considered him as henceforward free, and not likely to remember what had passed between them while they were both in exile.

Ivan's anger was roused. He said to her, "Princess Marie, you know that while you and yours are in exile, at no moment of my life will the thought that you are so, and the endeavour to procure your recall, be laid aside. After, that event, should it ever happen, I shall never cease to love you as I have hitherto loved you, with my whole heart and soul, but you shall then be perfectly free; and I am well aware that it is not likely that the Princess Marie Andréevna will ever think more of one so much beneath her in station as I am. And let me tell you now, knowing all your faults, knowing how hard it would be to secure your affections, I still can never love any other woman but you. Do you think that anything would induce me to leave you now, to give up the joy of sometimes sharing your troubles and your burdens, if it were not for the hope, however vain that hope may be, of gaining your recall from this horrible place? Otherwise, it would be torture to me to leave you."

This was not exactly a lover-like speech, for lovers seldom venture to allude to the faults of their mistresses, but it was very significant of the strong, frank, and determined character of the young man, and perhaps it was the very best mode that he could have adopted for subduing her.

The Princess moved towards him timidly, then threw her arms round him, and using the fondest expressions of love, vowed that she would never forget him in his absence, and would never marry any one but him. At this moment the lovers were interrupted by the sudden appearance on the scene of the two persons who of all that little community, would be to them the most unwelcome witnesses of their parting as lovers.

BOOK II.

———◆———

CHAPTER V.

AMONGST the exiles who dwelt in that little town of Pelem, was one of the name of Nariskoff.

He was a person of remarkable character. He had originally been a man of fortune, the lord of many serfs. He had also been a great philanthropist; and had, as a youth, for his father died early, sought to improve the condition of those serfs. Previously to any great change for good in the world's affairs, there are solitary instances, here and there, of persons who foresee the possibility of attaining the good thing; make premature attempts to attain it; and perish in the attempt. In this case it was not literally perishing, for Nariskoff did not die; but he lost his fortune, and, what was more to be regretted, he lost his faith and his hope in mankind. Few men become so sour as disappointed philanthropists.

Nariskoff's main and guiding theory in his early life was so remarkable a one, that it deserves mention here, for, with some modifications, it is as applicable at the present time as it was at that period. He used to say, that as long as the lower stratum of mankind was miserable, all the other strata would be miserable too. He would add : " Why all these strivings and strugglings in our own class, but that we fear that we ourselves, or our descendants, should fall down into that lowest class. We desire especially to keep them as far removed from that as possible ; and so we plan, and we plot, and we work, and we slave, and we contend with our fellow-men, and we worship

the great 'Emperor, Rouble', and we are miserable, all of us."

This, of course, is but a very partial view of
human affairs; but poor Nariskoff was entirely
possessed by it; and it may not altogether be
unworthy of notice, in an age when competition
of all kinds is idolized.

Nariskoff had, by no means, even in his earlier
and better days, been without great faults of
character. He was a very sensual man. Much
love for ourselves, and for self-enjoyment, often
goes hand in hand with considerable love for
others, especially for their material well-being.
Nariskoff, deceived and even injured by those
serfs whom he had tried to raise—mocked at by
his neighbours—scorned by his relatives, who
had even endeavoured to make him out a lunatic,
—and looked upon by the authorities as a
dangerous man—fell into deep disgrace, as
well as utter misfortune. He was, however,
a very witty and humorous person; and having given up all hope of benefiting "those
copious fools," as he was wont to call them,

" his fellow-creatures," and even having taken a dislike to them, he resolved, for the remainder of his life, to do little more than prey upon them.

A Timon, of a lower order than that which the great master of human character has depicted, Nariskoff did not retire into a desert; but, on the contrary, sought out the busiest haunts of men. His powers of entertainment made his presence acceptable at the tables of the great. Gradually he had become accustomed to his dependent condition, and his wit degenerated more and more into ill-natured personal satire, so that latterly before his exile, his company had been more sought from fear than from regard. Though, comparatively speaking, an obscure man, his obscurity had not saved him from exile. When Prince Serbatoff was banished, Nariskoff, being supposed to be an intimate friend of the Prince's, was, with him, condemned to exile. There was not one of the exiles who more deplored his lot than he did. He had become a thorough sensualist, and bitterly mourned over the loss of the rich viands and luxurious living for which he had bartered his wit in former days.

During his exile he had shown no particular gratitude to his former friend and benefactor, Prince Serbatoff. Indeed, he considered the Prince as the cause, however innocent, of his own exile, and was embittered against him on that account. He did not quarrel with the Prince : quarrelling was not Nariskoff's forte ; but he did not seek to do him any service, and indeed he rather avoided the Serbatoff family, fearing lest he might be called upon to aid the young Princess in her servile labours.

One friend, however, or rather one associate, this man had found among the dwellers of that little town. And this was a half-witted person of the name of Matchka. This poor creature was not an exile, but one of the original inhabitants of the town—perhaps a descendant of some exile. If there were any special reason that made Nariskoff attach himself to this simpleton, it was that he could put into Matchka's mouth the ill-natured sayings which he himself feared to utter.

It was the approach of Nariskoff and Matchka, that had suddenly been noticed by the lovers, and had not a little disconcerted them. Most of the inhabitants of the town had, at that time of the day, gone to their work; but Nariskoff, who somehow or other still continued to live upon his wits without work, and Matchka, who throve upon his folly, did not indulge in daily labour, and could afford time to observe other people, and to meddle in their affairs. Indeed, it was upon this meddling humour that they lived and prospered, as far as anybody could prosper in that region of misery.

Upon seeing these two men in the distance, the lovers immediately separated, the Princess going into her father's hut, and Ivan returning to the Duke of Courland's house.

It had been arranged that Ivan was to start that evening on his return to St. Petersburg. The scene at his departure was a very touching one. Almost every family of the exiles had prepared letters which they furtively entrusted to his care. But, more than that,—he was almost torn

to pieces by persons privately soliciting him to
aid their cause at Court. He had become a very
great man among them. No sooner had he begun
to listen to the story of some poor exile, who
was declaring his innocence of all plots against
any government, and vowing that he had always
felt the deepest attachment to the present Duchess
Regent and the Field Marshal, Count Münnich,
than, he, (Ivan) was forcibly carried off to some
other group to listen to a similar story and similar
protestations of duty and affection to the new
reigning powers. If any cynical observer, perfectly cognizant of the state of affairs at the
Russian Court, had been present, it would have
amused him to think how idle, nay, how injudi-
cious such protestations were, seeing that at this
very time, the chief conspirators who had deposed
the Regent from power, were now in bitterest
enmity with one another. By the time that Ivan
reached the capital, another revolution, or semi-
revolution, had occurred; and Count Münnich
was no longer in power.

During the remainder of the day of Ivan's

departure, the two lovers had no opportunity of meeting, except in the presence of other persons. And when he left the town, the crowd of applicants for favour who surrounded him, prevented the approach of her whose fond words at parting could, alone, have been of any comfort to him.

BOOK II.

—◆—

CHAPTER VI.

DISCOVERY OF THE DUKE OF COURLAND BY HIS
FELLOW-EXILES.

When the exiles who dwelt in Pelem, had
time to think of anything but themselves and their
hopes in reference to the letters which they had
entrusted to Ivan, they could not help noticing
that the mysterious man, (friend, or relative they
knew not) with whom Ivan had dwelt, had not
made himself visible on the occasion of the young
man's departure, and had not been present to
exchange a parting salutation with him.

This man became more than ever an object of

curiosity, and he was now occasionally obliged to make himself visible, for though the Starost of the village had received orders to supply him with food and fuel, there were occasions on which, from some trifling circumstance or other, he was obliged to leave his house in the daytime.

Nariskoff had naturally had his eye upon this mysterious stranger. He had shrewdly conjectured that he must be a person of some especial importance, to be favoured as he was; and Nariskoff was anxious to share the advantages which arose from this favour. He had before schemed to secure the liking of rich and great men, in order to sit at luxurious banquets; but now the humblest necessaries of life had become in that community objects of the most precious kind. Doubtless among savages there is as much refined flattery with an eye to choice feathers, shells, or wampum, as amongst civilized people to gain favours of the highest kind. Nariskoff had several times endeavoured to win an entrance into the two-storied house; but all his advances to its mysterious occupant had met with no shadow

of response. Nariskoff had therefore given up
this mode of procedure, and had determined upon
hostility to gain his ends.

It happened that one day at evening, the Duke,
feeling very solitary at home now that Ivan had
departed, had ventured out of his house. He
was still closely muffled up, and had devoted
himself to studying the means of disguising his
personal appearance. There were, unfortunately
for him, many of the exiles in the straggling
street at this moment. It was the day of a great
Russian festival; and these exiles, like all other
persons in their position, held very much to
ancient usages which reminded them of home
and former days. The little church was lighted
up; and the townsmen were gathered together
in groups waiting to welcome a procession of
priests and choristers, who were to enter the
church, when the service would begin.

The Duke, on perceiving the concourse that
he had come upon most unwittingly, for he took
no heed of festivals, and indeed had always been
a stranger in the land, made a movement to

return to his house. Then, thinking probably that this would excite increased suspicion, he went boldly forward in the direction towards the great forest that half-encircled the town. "Now," thought Nariskoff, "is my opportunity!"

Matchka was a devout believer in the Russian Church and its ceremonies, in which he was often allowed to take a humble part, and this was the poor half-witted man's chief delight. He could starve, or would, if he had any food, share it with his friend Nariskoff, whom he venerated; but not even Nariskoff could have persuaded him, upon any pretext, to absent himself from the least important ceremony of the Church.

Bitter, at that time, was the dislike of an orthodox believer in the Greek Church to a follower of the sect of Ruskolnicks.* Suddenly the thought flashed into Nariskoff's mind of what might be done to tear off the veil, as it were, from the mysterious man, by enlisting the foolish Matchka's bigotry for that purpose.

---

* Ruskolnick means 'divider' or 'sectarian.'

"Matchka," he said, "do you see that man going away from our great festival of Saint Alexander Newski? As I live, he is a Ruskolnick. You must prevent his going. We will know whether he is a Ruskolnick or not; and, if he is, his presence must no longer defile Pelem. You must insist upon seeing him face to face. We never have seen what he looks like."

This was quite sufficient inducement for Matchka to do what he then did. He ran after the Duke, and seized him by his cloak, crying out at the same time that he was a Ruskolnick. A violent altercation took place. The Duke endeavoured to force his way on. Matchka barred his progress.

Meanwhile, Nariskoff had rapidly moved from group to group, and had drawn their attention to the contest between the fool and the mysterious man. Nariskoff took Prince Serbatoff aside. "My little Father," he said, "is there no one of whom that man reminds you? He must be some one whom you would know, or he would not have bread and fuel found for him by the orders of the

Governor, while we have to toil for our scanty living."

The Prince, in general indifferent to all that surrounded him, thinking himself the greatest man amongst those exiles, who alone had never even turned his head to look at this new companion in misery, was compelled by Nariskoff's earnest entreaties to turn and regard him.

The contest between Matchka and the Duke had now proceeded from words to blows. They closed in their encounter; and, as they struggled together, the Duke's cloak, his furred cap, and some parts of his artificial disguisement were torn off.

"God in Heaven!" exclaimed the Prince, "it is the Duke of Courland—the Regent of yesterday—the accursed wretch to whom all our misery is due!"

From group to group the information spread like wildfire. At first there was doubt; but not for long, as many there had seen and trembled at the countenance of the Duke of Courland. Then there was wonder: then horror mixed with

fear, as of slaves who suddenly see their master
bereft of power, but still, from the tyranny of
custom, cannot believe it. Then there was a
general movement towards him; and he was at
bay with all his enemies—enemies who had for
years been nursing hatred towards him. Matchka
had now got the best of the encounter, and
remained at a few paces from the Duke, crying
out loudly that he was a Ruskolnick.

The greatness of mind which there was in
De Biron, did not desert him on this occasion.
He looked composedly around and said, " Yes, I
am the Duke of Courland, by right your Regent;
and what then ? "

The crowd were awed at first; but this awe did
not last long. The more violent of them sprang
upon him. So fierce and furious was their handling
of him, that his clothing was almost at once torn
to pieces. This would undoubtedly have been his
last moment of life, had not the priests and their
attendants, wondering at the neglect which their
entry into the church had met with, come out of
it again, and approached the scene of conflict.

With sturdy blows and violent denunciations, which no man ventured to return or gainsay, they forced their way towards the Duke's assailants, and imperatively demanded that he should be given up to them. Prince Serbatoff seconded their endeavours, and he was warmly aided by the Starost. Their joint commands were obeyed. The Duke, in a most miserable plight,—half-naked, bruised and bleeding—was delivered up to the priests, who led him to his own house, around which, till midnight, the ceremonies of the church being altogether forgotten, there was one wild, continuous howl of execration.

BOOK II.

CHAPTER VII.

THE NIGHTLY VISITOR TO THE DUKE OF COURLAND.

WITH the exception of those who were blind or bed-ridden, there was not a single person in the little community of exiles, who had not been a witness of the proceedings recounted in the last chapter. The Princess Marie was one of the maidens who assisted in the choir, and she had come out of the church with the priests, when they hurried forth to learn the cause of the disturbance. She had seen the man to whom all eyes had been directed in the plenitude of his power; and she could not but re-

member, that, at her first appearance at the
Russian Court, her chief desire had been to
know what *he* was like, who was the greatest
man at Court. She had been presented to him;
and was much gratified by the few kind words
which he had addressed to the daughter
of his colleague, whom he had not then determined to send to Siberia.

It was impossible for one, in whose mind was
much of poetry and romance, not to be affected
greatly when she beheld the same man dragged
to his house, wounded, bleeding and half naked,
a miserable spectacle to gods and men. Not
that her hatred was less; for the Princess had
inherited from her father an ample faculty for
hating.

Her first thoughts, however, were about Ivan;
and they were very bitter. She felt that she
had been deceived. She absolutely raged at the
thought that this young man, the devoted follower, for so she held him to be, of the arch-
enemy of her house, had gained her love without
revealing himself. In her first access of anger,

she did not pause to think that Ivan was bound
by the strictest ties of honour, not to disclose his
master's name; neither did she pause to conjecture that which had really been the truth,
namely, that Ivan had at first sought her society,
in order that he might aid her in her daily
domestic labours. He had, it is true, admired
her at a distance, when she first appeared at
Court. He had afterwards, on the downfall of
her family, constituted himself their unknown
protector. But, at the beginning of their intimacy at Pelem, it had never entered even into
his wildest dreams to imagine that he should
win her love, or should even attempt to do so.

The community of exile had not effaced that
difference of rank and station, which, in later
times, was maintained in the prisons of the
French revolution, where the noblesse still held
together, and when the difference of caste was
felt up to the very moment when the tumbril
was to convey to the guillotine the ill-assorted
batches of human victims.

But the love had come; and even, with her

present feelings of bitterness and almost of aversion, the Princess could not but own to herself, for she was one of those persons who never knowingly practised self-deception, that she loved Ivan, and only Ivan, and would continue to love him to the end of her days. She did not, however, hesitate in making a stern resolve to give him up. And it was with a feeling of indignation that she thought of the efforts he would be sure to make, to procure the recall of herself and her family. She hated to think of being under obligation to one who, as she thought, had so cruelly and basely deceived her.

It may be imagined with what expressions of triumph and joy the Prince described to his blind wife the scene which he had just witnessed, and the part which he himself had taken in it. Yet even he could not altogether omit throwing in some remarks which tended towards pity, when he dwelt upon the contrast of the Regent's former position and of his present condition. It might have been observed, that the

Prince had a cynical delight in speaking of De Biron as the Regent.

The poor blind lady, a deeply religious woman, could not help occasionally expressing her pity in such moderate terms as she ventured to use in her husband's presence; and, when she was alone with her daughter, she spoke with the fulness of commiseration which her own long-suffering had taught her.

Women have a great pity for physical suffering. It is a blessed thing that it is so. There are some amongst them who perhaps do not sympathize as much as men expect with the mental anxieties and sufferings of a man, and especially with his care about distant things—distant from home as it were, such as the great questions touching upon politics, religion, or the future hopes and prospects of the world. But, for present disaster of any kind and for physical suffering, women have a depth and keenness of pity and sympathy which is almost beyond the ken of the sterner partners of their lives.

It is well, for the understanding of the complicated history of Russia at this period, and also for the right understanding of this narrative, to state that De Biron's overthrow, however much personal gratification it might afford to people like the Prince, was not, politically speaking, a great cause for rejoicing to them. The friends of Menschikoff, Peter the Great's favourite, and notably those who had been employed by the late Empress Anne, were considered by the present Duchess Regent as her especial enemies; and the Regent's downfall was not a revolution which could affect them favourably.   Now the Prince was one of those persons; and, therefore, no word of congratulation passed among the members of this family with regard to their own future prospects by reason of the political changes which had occurred.

The Princess Marie passed an agitated and sleepless night. The turmoil of her soul was great. She was torn by emotions of the most opposite kind. Her love for Ivan—her wrath with

him—even contempt for him—her hatred for the
Duke of Courland—her pity for his abject condition—alternately occupied and ruled her mind.
At last she came to a determination, respecting
which it would be very difficult to assign all the
motives, good and bad, which led to it. One
motive must be candidly confessed. It was,
however, an after-thought. But it must be
owned that the Princess did think that what she
was about to do, would be a sort of triumph
over Ivan, and would serve to diminish the
weight of any obligation which either his past
or his future services to her family might impose
upon her. These after-thoughts of worldly
wisdom often occur, as attendants upon the most
generous actions, and are even used as an excuse
for performing those actions.

BOOK II.

—◆—

CHAPTER VIII.

THE DUKE'S COMFORTER.

WE must return to the Duke of Courland. His sufferings were great; but, strange to say, they were more of a physical than a moral kind. He had often anticipated in his mind the discovery that had just occurred, and its consequences, so that when the evil thing really did come, it neither surprised nor shocked him very much. He had, in fact, never hoped to escape with life when it should once be discovered who he was.

The Duke was a man of nice and delicate

habits who had loved luxury and splendour very much; and his cruelty to others had not rendered him less tender of his own person. He dressed his wounds as best he could, re-clothed himself, and laid himself down on the floor, for he feared lest, if he went to bed, he should there be surprised, in a most defenceless state, by an inroad of his enemies.

It was two or three hours after mid-night; and he was slumbering with the light and broken sleep which is the utmost that persons in pain and in great fear of peril can hope to enjoy, when he was awakened by a gentle knocking at the door of his house. He made no movement in response. The knocking continued. On reflection it seemed likely to him that the priests or the Starost of the village might be coming to him on a good errand, wishing to remove him secretly from the fury of the people.

He went softly to the roof of the house, and looked down. By the light of the moon, he saw that it was a woman, and, as it seemed to him, a young woman who was still gently knocking at the door. At first he thought that there might be some ambush, and that there were persons ready to rush in, if he should open the door to her. He gazed intently : he listened intently. There was nothing unusual to be seen or heard ; and the brilliancy with which the moon shone, was such as to light up every nook and corner near the house.

The Duke went down and admitted his visitor. He held up his lamp to her face as she entered ; but he did not recognize any countenance that he had ever known. In truth it would have been diffi-cult to recognize, in the imbrowned features, in the sordid dress, and in the marked lines of pur-pose which were now to be seen in the Princess Marie's countenance, the pallid, delicate, refined and splendidly attired young lady who had been introduced to him at Court.

" What are you come for ? " he exclaimed.

" To take care of you," she replied.

" Why ? " was his answer. " Are you a friend, or the daughter of a friend ? Are you sent by the priests, or by the Starost ? "

"No I am not: you must be ill, you are wounded, you are in pain; and it is my duty, as a woman, to care for you."

The Duke looked at her fixedly. He had not hitherto had a very good opinion of mankind. As far as he had known them, they had been chiefly servile adulators, or nascent conspirators. It was, perhaps, the first time in his life that he felt what possible worth there was in human nature. He shivered slightly, then took her hand, and felt the tears rise to his eyes, the pitying tears for himself, and a sort of sympathy with her sympathy for himself.

There was but little more said between them. She only remarked in business-like tones, that her time was short; and then, quite composedly, as if she had been as accustomed to dress wounds as a Sister of Mercy at a hospital, she unrolled some linen bandages which she had prepared.

So clumsily had the Duke dressed his own wounds, that the blood was slightly oozing from their bandages. He submitted himself entirely to her management, far more skilful than his own; and half an hour was spent before his wounds had been re-dressed, and every alleviation that she could give to his sufferings, had been rendered.

Before they parted, he again sought to know who she was. She declined to tell him. He seized her hand, and pressed it warmly. She withdrew it with evident repugnance. He was unable to flatter himself that there was any friendly feeling, or anything more than the merest woman-like pity in the service this girl had rendered to him. She only said, on leaving the house, "I will come again to-morrow night."

Notwithstanding her injunctions that he should not leave his position, he rushed to the door directly she had quitted it; but was not quick enough to discern which way she had taken; and he remained in utter ignorance of the dwelling of his benefactress.

Comforted in body, but not consoled in mind, the ex-Regent lay down upon the floor again.

Night after night the Princess Marie returned to render him similar services. By day he was safe, as the Starost of the village had placed a guard near the house; but little or no attention had, otherwise, been given to his sufferings. Indeed none cared whether he lived or died. The only desire of the priests and the Starost was that the Duke's death should not be caused by violence at the hands of his brother exiles.

There have been many strange conversations in the world; but perhaps none have been stranger than those which took place between the Princess Marie Andréevna Serbatoff and his Highness the ex-Regent of Russia.

He felt intuitively that she condemned him, and that she was probably one of those who had suffered from his indiscriminate cruelty. He sought to justify himself. He told her the story of his life. He enumerated the great things he had done, and the great things he intended to have done, for Russia.

Her replies, when any replies she made, were chilling. Once, and once only, she reminded him of a signal act of cruelty which he had authorized. He bowed his head, and made no answer. The Princess Marie felt at the moment how untrue she had been to the functions she had taken upon herself of a nurse to this wretched being; and she did not commit a similar fault again—at any rate during the height of his illness, and when any excitement might increase his feverish symptoms.

It would be tedious to recount the various conversations which took place between the Princess Marie and the Duke of Courland. It may suffice to relate the following one as being very significant of the characters of these two remarkable persons. The Princess Marie, woman-like, sought to do some good to the soul, as well as to the body of her patient. She had been bred up to think him a monster of iniquity, and was surprised to perceive few, if any, signs of repentance for his former cruelties.

The conversation turned, as she often contrived it should turn, upon the ways of managing men. It may be premised that the Princess, finding it awkward to be without a name for these occasions, had on a previous day told the Duke to call her Katerina. It was her mother's name.

The conversation which had begun in a playful way, about the difficulty of managing a sick man, had come to this pass, that they were in high dispute upon the vexed question, still remaining vexed for us, as to whether men were to be ruled by gentleness or severity.

"I do not see the use of so much knout," the Princess exclaimed; "it only hardens men."

"I do:" replied the Duke, "you would, I suppose, prefer the punishment of death?"

"I should prefer no punishment at all," rejoined the Princess somewhat nettled,—"no punishment at all for most of the so-called crimes which have been so severely punished in recent times."

"Did you know my private Secretary, Katerina? You must, I think, have seen him. A tall young man with fair hair? He used to sing with the priests."

"Rather innocent looking, if I recollect rightly," was her reply.

"Yes: innocent looking," said the Duke: "more so than some people who are wont to talk the same nonsense as he did. I remember—'twas that same night when the arch-villain, Münnich, stole upon me—that this youth was good enough (I own I asked for his opinion) to impart to me his views of government, and to inform me that my rule had been too severe. The young are always rebels—rebels at heart."

"Perhaps," replied the Princess, "it is because they are justly dissatisfied with the rule of their elders, and think that something better might be made of life than what they see around them.

"And is that 'better'" said the Duke, "to come by means of conspiracies and revolutions? Now listen to me, young woman, have you ever thought what a State is?"

"I don't know, my lord, that I have ever thought what statesmen like your Highness take a State to be; but it seems to my poor childish mind, that a State is not a very glorious thing, when it requires to be maintained by the constant use of the knout, the rack, the axe, and exile."

The Duke of Courland walked up and down the room several times in silence; and then with much energy of voice and manner addressed the Princess thus.

"There are millions of fellow-subjects in this State, that we are talking of. Every one of them has infinite desires. He would be all in all. It is only by the strong arm of the law suspended over him, that he is held for a moment from molesting his weaker neighbour. The State may be ever so rudely formed; but it has taken hundreds, perhaps thousands, of years to get it into any form whatever—to enable men to work together in something like peace, and to husband something for the future. If this be true of other States, it is pre-eminently true of Russia— of Russia, hardly yet rescued from the condition of wandering nomadic tribes. And all this you would upset upon the chance of making something better—you, with your juvenile wisdom, Katerina. Ivan, that is his name, was almost as wise as yourself."

The Princess felt that she blushed as she heard

their names so brought together. Had Ivan told the ex-Regent anything? Surely not, she said to herself.

The Duke continued. "You brush away, in your housewifely neatness, a spider's web. It is well—but could you make the thing again? Not even that. And yet you are sure you could reconstruct, and greatly improve upon the delicate but strong net-work of interwoven webs of custom, law, manners, lineage and history, of which a State is formed, and by which its people are kept in harmony. Unravel it, or destroy it, you can, if rulers are fools enough to let you do so."

Again there was silence for a minute or two, for the Princess, perceiving the fierce irony of the ex-Regent's mood, did not dare to interrupt him. "Why, girl," he resumed, "did I not, as I have told you before, raise towns, build bridges, keep rivers within due bounds, bring men of science to the capital, and continually promote that civilization, which had been the dream—a noble one, I must say—of that barbarian Peter? And then, that smooth-faced youth and you, for I can see what you are always hinting at, would condemn the Duke of Courland because he sent a few thousand useless and troublesome people into exile, and so saved the State."

In almost every Russian room there is, in one of the corners of it, a rude picture of the Almighty or of our Saviour, with a lamp burning under it.

The only reply the Princess made to this tirade, was by pointing to this picture and saying, "Were those the means that He would have used—that He enjoined?"

"I did not rule over Christians," replied the Duke.

"I thought," said the Princess, "that the orthodox Greek Church was Christian."

" You thought so, did you, my innocent Katerina: some thousands of years hence, the mass of mankind may be Christian, for aught I know, —though I think it unlikely; but it is not Christian now, and must be ruled as it was in Pagan times. Boys and girls may dream; but it is men who have to rule. That is the answer I have to make to you—you cowards—as well as to her." Here the Duke looked wildly about him.

This was the first time that the Princess had any suspicion, and now it was but a faint suspicion, of the Duke's remorse; for she could perceive that he was addressing some imaginary beings. She began to fear for his sanity; and, as rapidly as possible, endeavoured to change the subject, requesting to see how his wounds were progressing. The Duke perceived her aim, and fearing lest by his violence he should have frightened her, said no more upon these dangerous topics; but submitted his wounds for her inspection; and for the short time that remained previously to her departure, endeavoured to make the conversation light and lively, and so to efface the painful impression which he saw that he had made upon her mind. Few persons were more skilled than the Duke of Courland in all the arts which go to make pleasant companionship. It was not, however, without many misgivings as regarded his sanity, and some fear as to any

future visit, that the Princess Marie took her
departure that morning as daylight began to
appear.

The Duke of Courland, as is the case with
many men whose whole lives are spent in the
endeavour to rise in the world, had never really
known what love was. He had never profoundly
admired, or greatly respected, any woman. He
had been the late Empress's favourite; and, as
many persons believed, her favoured lover. He
had married a daughter of one of the nobles of
Cawland; and his marriage had not been an
unhappy one. Neither had he failed, in earlier
days, to have considerable affection for the
Empress, who had been constant to him in
almost slavish devotion. But he had never
known what it was to lose all thought of himself
in his admiration for any woman; to idealize
all her perfections; and to think that converse
with her was the greatest blessing this earth
could give.

Something of that kind he began to feel now;
and yet it was not exactly love that he felt, at

least in its ordinary sense. The Duke was a
very shrewd man, and knew that there was
nothing like love possible either on her side,
or on his. He fully recognized that it was only
from pity, that she had devoted herself to serve
and tend an outcast, such as he was. He
worshipped her from a distance, as it were;
and the improvement in the character of the
man, might be seen, in that he it was who
urged her, night after night, not to return to
him again, at peril to herself, though he felt that
almost the only hope or comfort left to him in
life, was the returning presence of this maiden.

If we were to analyse what were the Princess
Marie's thoughts and feelings, we should find
that her hatred for the ex-Regent had greatly
diminished. It is almost impossible for a man,
it is certainly impossible for a woman, to serve
and tend any human being, without acquiring,
though almost unconsciously, a certain liking for
the creature so served and tended. And the
Princess, though she possessed a character of
some sternness, was not superior to her sex in

this respect. She began to feel much less of disgust, and somewhat even of regard, for one, to whom she had rendered such great service.

During this time remarkable events were occurring at the Court of Russia, which had much influence upon the fate and fortunes of most of the persons who were actors in this story; and these events must now be related.

BOOK III.

BOOK III.

—◆—

CHAPTER I.

THE PRINCESS ELIZABETH'S CHARACTER AND POSITION
—THE DUCHESS OF BRUNSWICK MADE REGENT—
LESTOCQ AND THE FRENCH AMBASSADOR LA CHÉ-
TARDIE—THEIR CONSPIRACY.

THERE are those who contend that the march of events would have been all the same whether certain forcible individuals who, moreover, have had the opportunity of bringing their powers into action, had lived or not. This, however, seems but fond pedantry to those, who, on the other hand, think that all history is, for the most part, little else than a series of biographies of eminent persons.

To this latter class of the students of history, it must ever appear strange that a certain eminent person at the Russian Court had, hitherto, during the various changes of supreme power, made so little figure, and had been apparently of so little account.

This person was the Princess Elizabeth, daughter of Peter the Great and of Catharine his second wife.

There was no Salic law in Russia.

The Princess was known to be a woman of considerable ability, inheriting many of her father's great qualities ; and yet on every occasion she is unaccountably passed over. It is not to be supposed that her illegitimacy (for she was born during the lifetime of Peter's first wife) was, alone, a sufficient disqualification. The most plausible solution that occurs, is, that, in the early part of her life, she was utterly unambitious, and indeed was wholly devoted to pleasure of all kinds. During the greater part of the reign of the Empress Anne, the Princess Elizabeth had remained perfectly quiet ; had never meddled with State affairs; nor, apparently, had taken any interest in them. She probably thought that the Crown would quietly devolve upon her after the death of that Empress.

It was not until the present Duchess Regent, who was only a grand-daughter of Peter the Great's elder brother, married Anthony Ulric, Duke of Brunswick, that the Princess began to form a party.

This she did with the utmost secrecy. She might still have been chosen by Biron to succeed the Empress Anne, but for the circumstance of an infant child being born to the Duchess of Brunswick.

The infancy of this child gave a pretext for Biron's appointment to the Regency; and, doubtless, induced him to use his predominant influence in favour of the choice which the Empress finally made of this infant as her suc-cessor.

The Grand Duchess of Brunswick, now the Regent, committed a great political error, though a very natural one, when she joined with Münnich

in his conspiracy against Biron. By the Duke
of Courland's downfall the Grand Duchess was
deprived of the only statesman who could have
saved her, and assured the kingdom to her infant
son. It is true that another statesman was left
to her—Count Ostermann. But his infirmities,
though sometimes exaggerated by him, and made
most useful to account for his absence on any
critical occasion, were real, and would not allow
him to supply the place of the vigorous and
suspicious Duke of Courland.

On the other hand, the Princess Elizabeth had
two persons who were devoted to her interests,
and were very ready to embark in conspiracy, if
not well-skilled in conducting it. They were
both of them Frenchmen. One was Lestocq, the
surgeon of her household; the other was the
Marquis De la Chétardie, the French ambassador.

Ambassadors in those days did not hesitate to
interfere, as partisans, in the internal affairs of
the countries they were accredited to; and, it is
said, that La Chétardie had instructions from his

own Court to foment any kind of internal discord in Russia, with a view to prevent her from becoming troublesome to the rest of Europe, and especially to France.

Lestocq was of French extraction, the son of French exiled Protestants; but his whole bearing partook more of the general character of his compatriots than of that of his religious brethren. He had been originally in Peter the Great's own household; and it is said that he was dismissed by that Emperor on account of his unmitigated debauchery. The existence of any such squeamishness on the part of that monarch, may be doubted. A more probable conjecture is, that Peter had discovered Lestocq's intriguing disposition and dangerous character; and that the debaucheries served as a pretext for dismissal—the more so as Lestocq had been admitted into the Princess Elizabeth's household in the same capacity as that which he had filled in her father's.

Lestocq's frivolous manners, his love of talking, and his careless mode of speaking about everything, were no doubt greatly in his favour, as a

means of concealment for his dangerous designs.
He was, however, greatly suspected by some of
the ministers of the Grand Duchess Regent, and
by the foreign ambassadors who were not in the
interest of France. Between the French ambassador, La Chétardie, and Lestocq, there was
great intimacy, and constant communication.
The two conspirators took care never to meet
either at the French ambassador's Palace, or at
the Palace of the Princess Elizabeth; but they
had some obscure place of meeting, in which a
conspiracy was being formed to subvert the
Duchess Regent, to alter the succession of the
throne, and to place the Crown upon the head of
the Princess Elizabeth.

In addition to these two devoted friends, the
Princess had her own dissembling spirit; and
she was profound in dissimulation.

The Duchess Regent, on the contrary, was an
indolent, good-natured, placable woman, who, so
long as she could shut herself up in her private
apartments with her infant child and with
her favourite, Juliana de Mengden, was con-

tented to let the world go on very much as it pleased.

For the first few months after Biron's exile, the Duchess Regent and the Princess Elizabeth were apparently upon the best terms of harmony. Gradually, however, mutual distrust arose; and it might have raised the most serious suspicions in any other mind but that of the indolent Duchess Regent, to find that the Princess never went to see her, except upon days of ceremony, or when, from strict etiquette, she was obliged to pay some visit to the Court. Her presence at that Court was rendered more irksome and displeasing to her by reason of a project which had been formed by the reigning powers to unite the Princess in marriage to a brother of the Grand Duke of Brunswick.

In order to further the conspiracy, for Elizabeth had now determined to conspire, money was wanting, and this the French ambassador liberally supplied. He was also most useful in guiding Lestocq, with whom he had many secret conferences.

The aim of the conspirators was, that the revolution should be caused by the soldiery; and
the Princess Elizabeth began by gaining over
several of the soldiers of the Preobraskenski
regiment. Her principal agent in this matter
was a man of better education than most of
his fellows. His name was Grunstein. He
had been a merchant, had become bankrupt,
and had enlisted in the Preobraskenski regiment. By degrees he gained over twenty-nine
other Grenadiers to become members of the
plot.

The ambassadors of the great Powers, who
were hostile to France, or who, at any rate, did
not take the same view of Russian affairs as the
French ambassador, did not fail to warn the
Duchess Regent of her danger.

Lestocq was a giddy, vain man; and he had
been heard to say, on some occasion, at a café,
that there would soon be seen great changes in
St. Petersburg. Count Ostermann, who was
well supplied with intelligence by his spies, re-
ported this talk to the Duchess Regent, who,

however, only laughed at it. It cannot be said that the conspiracy was well managed. There were now many persons having strong suspicions that such a project was on foot; and, besides, anything that is absolutely confided to more than two or three human beings, cannot well be called a secret.

Still the Princess Elizabeth delayed to strike a a bold stroke; and, indeed, when it was pressed upon her to do so, she always found some good reason for delay. At length, however, it was resolved, with her consent, that on the 6th of January, 1742 (Twelfth Day, when all the troops in garrison at St. Petersburg are paraded on the ice of the Neva), the deed should be done. The Princess was to go there, and was to make a speech to her regiment of Preobraskenski, declaring her claim to the Empire. They would no doubt receive this speech with acclamation; the other regiments would follow their example; and thus the conspiracy was sure to be successful.

This determination was taken at least a month

before it was to be put into execution; but certain events occurred which greatly tended to confirm the resolve of the Princess Elizabeth, and to hasten her action. It was about this time that she learnt that the Grand Duchess had been advised to declare herself Empress. It was also about this time that certain regiments stationed at St. Petersburg were ordered to join the army in Sweden. In these regiments were many adherents to the cause of the Princess. Neither, however, of these important and untoward circumstances would probably have sufficed to make the Princess act swiftly and resolutely, as long as the Grand Duchess herself did not make a move in the game. She was repeatedly warned of the existence of some conspiracy. The Marquis De Botta, ambassador from the Queen of Hungary, addressed her in these solemn words :—" Your Imperial Highness has declined assisting the Queen my mistress, notwithstanding the alliance between the two Courts ; but as there is now no remedy for that, I hope that, with the assistance of God, and of our other allies, we shall get out of our difficulties : but, at least, madam, do not at present neglect the taking care of yourself. You are on the brink of a precipice. In the name of God, save yourself! Save the Emperor! Save your husband !"

Even these emphatic words seem to have produced little or no impression, at the time, on the torpid mind of the Grand Duchess who remained perfectly inert.

BOOK III.

———◆———

CHAPTER II.

IT was in the depth of winter at St. Petersburg, and the time was evening, when a middle-aged gentleman might be seen making his way on foot through some back streets to a low kind of café, which was situated on the banks of the Neva.

He did not seem the kind of person who would, be likely to frequent such places of amusement. His furs were of the costliest, and his dress altogether was particularly well cared-for. He walked with a jaunty air, and dandled his cane in such a dainty fashion as might have given our great poet Pope the idea of Sir Plume.

> " Sir Plume of amber snuff-box justly vain,
> And the nice conduct of a clouded cane."

Notwithstanding his jaunty air, this fine gentleman did not seem thoroughly at ease. He walked down the middle of the streets, and frequently turned to see whether any one was following him. Then he would gaily hum a French air, and recommence his walk. Except on account of this occasional manifestation of suspicious vigilance, he would not in the least degree have fulfilled the idea which most men have of a conspirator—certainly not of a most dangerous conspirator. Good Heavens! upon what insignificant people the greatest affairs of this world often turn, as upon a pivot. The future destiny of Russia was to be much affected by this man, and even by his proceedings this evening. Changes of dynasty, changes of policy, Crimean wars, and other events still more important, were trembling in the balance; and it was for this man, unconsciously, to decide which way the balance should incline.

It was Lestocq, whose position in the household 'of Elizabeth and whose part in the projected conspiracy have been already described.

After many turnings and windings, the light-hearted French gentleman found his way to the café, and entered it. At the moment he entered, there was one of those curious contests in song, not uncommon among the Russian peasants and artisans, in which, indeed, men of a higher station were glad to join, sometimes as listeners, and sometimes even as competitors for the prize.

At that moment a peasant was singing a song of a rustic kind, representing the charms of the country, and his own sorrow at the falseness of his Arina. Rendered in prose, it ran thus :—

None of this noise, and turmoil and hurry: none !
No darkness of tall streets, and tumult of waggons: none !
But peace on the hills, and peace in the valleys,

Peace by the sunny stream that silently glides on ;
In the isba* is rest too, the bees round it humming.

Sweeter than all is the mid-day sleep in the forest,
By my side Arina watching ;
I awake, and find my Arina.

Broad are the heavens there, and the sky is wide open,
But not broad enough for the sorrow of men to be lost in.
Hearts are sad by Lena the still, as in Moscow the
      noiseful.

My tears flow with the river,
My sighs are borne upon the breeze ;
No bird so sorrowfully sings
As with me to partake of my sorrow.

Sadder than all is the mid-day sleep in the forest.
The false one no more by me watching ;
I awake, but Arina is not there.
          No, no, never more,
          Never more, Arina.

After the song had ended, there was a sound
of applause ; and while it was being decided who
should be the next singer, and suggestions were
being made from all parts of the room as to

* *Isba*, a cottage.

what he should sing, Lestocq took aside a
gloomy-looking man, dressed as a corporal of
the Preobraskenski regiment, and conversed
earnestly with him. This was Grunstein.

Snatches of the conversation might have been
heard. For instance, Lestocq spoke frequently
of a certain high festival of the Russians, called
the Consecration of the Waters of the Neva,
which was to occur in about a month's time.

"Too late, too late," muttered the gloomy
Grunstein. "We are ready if you are. Why
this delay?"

The replies of Lestocq, which were uttered in
a soothing tone, seemed to point out that some
woman's irresolution was the cause of the delay;
and the gay Frenchman broke out in a louder
tone into a general invective against women,
which was overheard, and was laughingly as-
sented to by many male voices, for there were
very few women present.

Then began the song of the next singer, a
humble lay, but sung with great feeling. It began thus:—

Far off in the forest rose the wreaths of smoke,
While sweetly a voice the glad echoes awoke ;
'Twas Netka sitting by the flames so bright,
Her dark hair glowed in the yellow light ;
>
>And ever as she sang,
>The woods around her rang ;
>And from the trees above,
>The nightingale and dove
>Now listened as entranced,
>And now the melody enhanced,

For the song was love, love, love.

After the song had ended, there was again a pause, while a new rival was sought for to the two preceding contenders for the prize.

During the interval several privates of the Preobraskenski regiment (this café was a favourite haunt of theirs) gathered round Lestocq and Grunstein ; and there was much gesticulation, and much dissatisfaction expressed by these soldiers, which, evidently, Lestocq and Grunstein sought to allay. Then came a song sung by one who seemed to be of a better station than that of the preceding singers. The words of the song appeared to be such as would have been more suitable to a more refined audience. This was the first stanza.

Whate'er in life that's beautiful I see,
　　Heroic deed, or noble word,
　　The triumph of the pen or sword,
　　I think of thee.
These are but images to me,
Full of thy beauteous memory.

This song was vociferously applauded; and it was evident, that if the audience had then had to adjudge the prize, this singer would have gained it. He, however, while there was much noisy dispute as to who should be the next singer, stole away, and was probably afterwards never recognized as the great singer who became the first tenor at the opera, and was eventually celebrated not only in Russia, but throughout Europe. He had come, from a strange fancy to see whether he could sway that audience, before he made his *debut* at the Opera; and he went away very well satisfied with his success.

It was generally felt by the company, that the soldiers should now do something to distinguish themselves, and should not merely be listeners.

To say the truth, the artisans and peasants

thought that they should have an easy victory,
for it was two of their especial favourites who
had hitherto come forward, and it was now
noticed that the third singer had left the
room.

After some whispering amongst the soldiers, a
young man of the regiment was made to come
forward, not without some reluctance on his
part. It might have been noticed, that both
Lestocq and Grunstein were much averse to any
song being sung by a soldier; but they were
not able to control the wishes of the other men
of the Preobraskenski regiment and of the
general company.

The song which the young soldier sang, was
rather a vague affair, enumerating at some
length the various merits and graces of the
Princess Elizabeth. The military poet who
composed it, had not confined his genius within
narrow bounds. The burden of it, however,
was sufficiently inspiriting, and, certainly very
distinct and outspoken.

Petrovna, our darling, the friend of the brave,
The foe of all those who would Russia enslave ;
    To thee our hopes have fled,
    For thee our blood we'll shed,
    Thy enemies, we'll strike them dead,
Petrovna, our darling, the friend of the brave!

It is not surprising that Lestocq and Grunstein should have endeavoured to prevent the singing of this song, which went so far to disclose their wishes and their purposes. It was amusing, however, to note the different characters of the two men. Grunstein maintained a moody silence, looking more morose than ever, whereas the genial Frenchman could only maintain his reticence during the refrain of the first verse, but joined in it most heartily and loudly when it came to be sung in chorus a second time.

After a little more of whispered conference between the two principal conspirators, Lestocq took his departure from the café; and when again in the frosty air, might still be heard humming, in lower tones, the refrain :

    " To thee our hopes have fled,
    " For thee our blood we'll shed,

" Thy enemies, we'll strike them dead,
" Petrovna, our darling, the friend of the brave ! "

The only prudence shown by this most jovial
of conspirators, was, that he made an immense
circuit, going up and down various streets needlessly, as if he had lost his way, before he
ventured to enter, by a little gate at the river-
side, the palace of his mistress, the Princess
Elizabeth.

BOOK III.

——◆——

CHAPTER III.

IN the meanwhile, was there no person besides the government spies, their ministerial employers, and the foreign ambassadors hostile to France, who was well aware of this conspiracy, and most anxious to thwart it? To answer this question, it is necessary to revert to the eventful story of the life of Ivan de Biron.

A miserable creature is an animal that has lost its master and its way, and is wandering about the streets of a great town, exhausting itself by fruitless efforts to discover whom and what it has lost. Another deplorable being, is one, who, in a strange land, is friendless, and does not know the language. There was a man in such a position, a clever self-reliant man when at home, who sat down upon the steps of a cathedral and fairly wept. For, as he told his friends when he got home, he felt like a wild beast. But neither of these sad conditions is much more, if at all more, wretched than that of a man, who, returning from exile, finds that all his former friends have partaken his fate, and that all his acquaintances shun him as being still "suspect."

This last condition was that of Ivan, on his return from Siberia. The members of the Biron family, and the principal adherents of the banished Duke of Courland, were still in exile, or were imprisoned in the Imperial fortresses. To whatever house Ivan directed his steps, he found strange faces at the door, and learnt that the former occupants were bereft of home, and fortune. Common acquaintances endeavoured to avoid recognizing him; and, when obliged to do so, passed quickly by on the other side.

A small sum of money had been given him immediately upon his being brought back by his escort to St. Petersburg; but no further notice was taken of him by the government, and he was left to find his own living as best he might.

It was in a most disconsolate mood, that Ivan roamed about the streets of that city; or, as sometimes happened, stayed all day long in his miserable lodgings, cowering over his stove, and thinking, what must be the end for him, when his small resources should be exhausted. Employment of any kind he could not obtain. His woe-begone appearance went much against him, especially as he could give no satisfactory account of his antecedents, and had a very lame story to tell, when asked about his former employment, and his former master. Once trusting to the good-natured face of an employer, Ivan had told the true story of his former life. It was to a printer, who was sometimes employed by government. This man's good-nature vanished instantly. He absolutely shuddered with affright, and bade Ivan quit the place directly. " A Biron indeed ! I wonder at his audacity. I hope that nobody saw him enter." Ivan, for several days, was too much disheartened to make any further effort of this kind. Starvation came nearer and nearer to him.

One evening, not long after his interview with the master-printer, Ivan, still wandering, aim-lessly, about the streets, was attracted by the sound of music, and entered the café before described as the favourite haunt of the Preo-braskenski regiment. It was that very evening when Lestocq visited the café; and Ivan was a witness of all the strange proceedings that went on during that night. These proceedings could not fail to make much impression upon one, who had been employed as the Duke of Courland's private secretary, who had been versed in un-ravelling conspiracies, and who had been accustomed daily to receive the reports of Biron's secret police.

From the café, Ivan went into the streets. He did not care to go home early. His lodgings, indeed, were little of a home for him; and he passed more and more of his time as the vagabonds in great towns pass theirs. He began to be nearly as well-informed as they are, of the nooks of shelter which are so serviceable to them; and, when taking refuge with other vagabonds from a sudden snow-storm, under the portico of some palace which in former days, he had, perhaps, entered as a guest, he would say to himself with bitter irony : " Benevolent beings, these nobles ! they doubtless built these porticoes for us." His young blood resisted the fearful coldness of that season ; and, indeed, there was a fever in his veins—a fever bred of ruined hopes, of hopeless love, of disappointed ambition—which made him almost insensible to external influences.

There was a great party that night at the Winter Palace ; and, in an open space between the palace and the Neva, there was a small crowd of people watching the arrival of the sledges. However cold it may be, there will be women of the lower classes anxious to see how women of the higher classes are dressed. The gypsies, from whom no festivities could be concealed, were in this open space; and it happened that they were the same band of gypsies which had given to the disguised Duke of Courland that information by their significant songs, which, if it had added to the wariness, as it did to the despondency of the Duke, would have preserved him from his downfall.

The beautiful Azra recognized Ivan; and the girl's heart was full of pity for him.

It must be recollected that, as said before, no persons of that time were better acquainted with political events, both those which had happened, and those which were likely to happen, as these bands of fortune-telling gypsies. They were a kind of police, acting for themselves, desirous of information solely that they might impose upon their dupes; and their intelligence, gained without any party prejudice, for they were strangers

in the land, and despised equally all parties in
the State, was often more trustworthy than the
reports which were made to the authorities by
hirelings.

It would have greatly shocked Lestocq and the
astute French ambassador, La Chétardie, if they
could have known that they were hardly more
cognizant of all the details of their projected
conspiracy, than were these almost outlaws, the
gypsies. It might have rendered the Princess
Elizabeth less inclined to waver in her decision,
if she, too, had been made aware of this
fact.

It may appear surprising, that the knowledge,
possessed by such persons, should not have been
made more direct use of by them for their own
purposes. But these outlawed beings had the
greatest aversion to connecting themselves in
any way with any transaction which might bring
them within the clutches of the law. They had
uniformly found that whenever they had concerned themselves with such transactions, their
part in them had been to suffer from the knout

and the rack; and that no gratitude had been displayed in return for any information they had given. They were an empire within an empire; and, as a general rule, their fealty to their own chiefs prevented any of the minor persons taking independent action.

On this evening the gypsies sang many of their favourite songs—songs adapted to the class of persons by whom they were surrounded. The usual business of fortune-telling went on; and Azra, as before, being a general favourite with the lower orders at St. Petersburg, was sent out of the gypsy circle by the chief, to take a prominent part in the proceedings.

She, without any direction from the chief, singled out Ivan, and sought to be allowed to tell him his fortune. The youth, influenced by the idleness of the moment, and also being curious to see whether the girl would repeat the story of his future fortunes in the same words which she had used on the former occasion, crossed her palm with one of the few coins still left to him; and was prepared to listen, not without a certain anxiety, for Ivan was not free from the superstitions of his time and his nation, to what she would tell him. He thought to himself "what can she invent to mitigate the fortunes of such an outcast wretch as I am. She will not remember me."

Now Azra did not know who Ivan was, but she did remember him, and she recollected that he had been in the company of the Duke of Courland on that eventful day when they had sought to give his Highness a warning of his coming fate. It surprised her much to find that Ivan was still in the land of the living, or, at least, that he was not partaking the exile to which she and all her tribe knew well that the Duke of Courland had been condemned. She had often found herself thinking, with pity, of this young man, wondering what his fate had been, and how he had borne it. She augured favourably, to some extent, of the young man's fortunes, from the fact of his being at St. Petersburg; but, at the same time, with the quick apprehensiveness of her race, she noted the signs of depression, almost of despair, which were clearly visible in his countenance. Moreover, the general air of poverty and neglect, which his dress and personal appearance manifested, were not lost upon her.

She began by telling him the usual story, the one familiar to the skilled tellers of fortunes; and in substance, though not in words, it was very nearly the same that she had told before. Then in figurative language, she said that the sky was darkened with black clouds, and that it almost touched the earth—his earth; and that there was no room for the light of love and joy between the black clouds and one whom they thus over-shadowed. Still, she maintained, that, though there was much adversity in the present moment, and the line of trouble had become much stronger, all hindrances would in the end be overcome; that he would be a great man (here she paused for some moments); and that, when he was this great man, he would never think more of the poor gypsy girl who now held his hand in hers, and commanded the stars for him. "But," she said, "if you would assure that fortune, you must meet me to-morrow morning, on

the bridge near St. Isaac's Church, at six o'clock.
I will tell you something, it may be only a dream,
which will give you back friends and fortune, and
love, and everything. You will come ?" His
eyes said, "Yes." Thereupon she withdrew
hastily into the circle; and the gypsies sang
that choral song, which was a never-failing
favourite with the people of Russia, the burden
of which runs thus :—

> Laugh who that may,
> Play, let him play,
> Drink, drink away;
> For to-morrow,
> May come sorrow;
> Then lose not, and fret not,
> The joys of to-day.

BOOK III.

—◆—

CHAPTER IV.

AZRA'S LOVE.

IVAN shared the prejudices of those amongst whom he had been brought up; and he looked upon the gypsies as a hostile race, specially inimical to all persons who had settled pursuits in his adopted country. But there was something in the young gypsy's earnestness which had deeply affected him; and, besides, he said to himself, "I am a vagabond now, and must not scorn fellowship with other vagabonds."

On the ensuing morning, he was the first to
make his appearance on the bridge, which had
been the appointed place of interview.

Love at first sight is not a thing unknown in
any country or in any class. It is not betraying,
unkindly, the sentiments of Azra, to admit that
during a sleepless, watchful night, she had felt
somewhat of a strange and unaccustomed feeling,
which, if not first love, might at least be called
first liking, for the young man whose manifest
depression had, at the outset, only excited her
pity. She would have given much, had much
been in her power to give, that that part of her
fortune-telling, should not have been true, which
made Ivan already in love with another girl.
" I am sure," she said to herself, " she is very
unkind to him, or he would not look so miserable.
I hate her. Still, I will give him that intelligence
which may ensure his welfare."

The poor girl even pictured to herself, how she
would join with the others in singing the bride-
song under his window, when he should marry
the young Russian lady whom she feared he was

in love with, but still had some hope that counter-acted that fear.

Ivan had not been three minutes on the bridge, before Azra made her appearance. The clock of a neighbouring church had just struck six; and not a human being was visible, either in the precincts of the church, or in the adjacent square of the Admiralty, but this young man and this young maiden. The magnificent church of St. Isaac's and the long buildings of the Admiralty, came forth distinctly to view. The golden dome of the one, and the golden spire of the other, rose up against the blue vault of heaven, and shone with brilliancy; for, early as it was, the moonlight, reflected from the clear sky above and from the bright snowy plains below, equalled the hazy beams of the risen sun as seen at mid-day in the cities of other northern climes we know of.

After the first greeting, Azra said timidly, "Was it all true then that I told you?"

"How can I tell, my dear? "Ivan replied. "It is not for me to foresee the future, but for you."

"Ah! But about the past?"

"I cannot say that it was altogether untrue."

The gypsy girl shuddered, but in a moment excused herself, saying, "We come from the East you know, from warmer, truer suns; and your northern air bites us strangers more spitefully than it does you."

Then she left him, and walked up and down by the frozen river-side, looking at the ice-bound Neva wistfully, as if it knew the secrets of men's and women's hearts, and might, if not controlled, betray hers.

This poor girl felt something now, which, heretofore, had been totally foreign to her. The young men of her tribe had sought her love in their rude way; but she had repelled their advances with a feeling alike of disgust and apprehension. Marriage, as seen among the elders of her tribe, had not presented itself to her in a very favourable light. In a word, she had not hitherto known what love was. In a moment she had felt it, or something very like it, for this stranger; and those depths of affection,

which are covered over by a thin crust in every
woman's soul, were disclosed. And she looked
down into them, as it were; and knew, with the
quick perception of that Orient race, that she
loved this youth; and that, as she then thought,
life for her without him would be desolation.

One question more, returning to the bridge,
she asked; and it was a bold one: "Does *she*
love you?"

Not even when sharply taken to task by his
imperious master, not in the whole course of his
official life, had Ivan ever felt that so difficult a
question had been put to him.

Azra looked up into his face, as if she expected
a plain and direct answer to this simple question;
and, though he saw an expression in her eyes,
which almost forbade him from answering the
question truthfully, and though it is a bold thing
to delare that any woman loves you, he did
muster up courage to answer truthfully, and to
say, "I think she does: I do believe she does."

The eyes of Azra sank beneath his gaze; and,
after a moment, she left him again, and walked

two or three times up and down by the banks of the Neva.

What great resolves are rapidly taken by us much-suffering mortals! All that the greatest thinker of our times has said about "renunciation," and about its being the greatest feat of which human nature is capable, was imaged forth, and illustrated by the thoughts which then passed through the innocent mind of that gypsy girl. We may live with the coarsest surroundings, as this poor child had done; but the great trials, the great conflicts of human existence, lie before the humblest and the poorest, as well as before the most self-sufficing and the grandest of the human race.

The gypsy girl looked upwards, as if to derive some guidance from those stars, which she believed concerned themselves so much with human affairs, even with such poor affairs as her own. Her gaze was not a prolonged one; and a few minutes only had passed, before she had come to the determination to make one of those sacrifices of self, which great poets celebrate in their finest verses, but which the self-sacrificers mostly conceal in their own breasts, thus completing the sacrifice by silence. She had resolved, at her own great peril, to give him fully that intelligence which yesterday she had only intended to hint at, and which would make his fortune at the Russian Court, and give to his arms that other girl whom she, her rival, would not, and could not believe would ever love him as she did.

The enormous danger which she ran from divulging, without the permission of her chief, any of the secrets possessed by her tribe, did not weigh much with her, so thoroughly had all-powerful love conquered selfish fear. The trial for her had been when she thought that the young man's fortune thus assured, would also ensure the triumph of his love—for another.

Again she approached Ivan, and, after looking cautiously around, she conveyed to him in a few whispered sentences the information, already known to our readers, of the conspiracy that was already so far advanced towards its final issue.

Ivan, at first, affected not to believe her story.

She reminded him of the truthfulness and the deep meaning of those hints which their tribe had darkly given to his companion, the Duke of Courland, on the first occasion of their meeting.

She also added such further details, that Ivan could no longer affect to doubt the truth of her intelligence. And it was finally agreed between them, that she should keep him well-informed of all that was going on, and, for that purpose, should meet him on the following day at the same hour, and at the same place.

BOOK III.

———◆———

CHAPTER V.

THIS chapter must begin with the correction of a statement that was made in a preceding one. It was stated that Ivan had been present at the Preobraskenski Café on the same evening that Lestocq was there. Further consideration shows that this could hardly have been the case. Ivan was at the café more than once; but a comparison of the dates would almost prove that he could not have been there on that special occasion, for he had several interviews with Azra after the first one, and these must have occurred some days before Lestocq's visit to the café. At any rate Ivan's suspicions could not have been first aroused by what he saw and heard at that café.

The perplexity into which Ivan's mind was thrown by Azra's intelligence, was extreme. What course should he take? Which cause should he adopt? He had no longer the slightest doubt of the existence of the plot; and that, one way or other, it would come to a final issue in a few days' time. Already skilled, far beyond what might have been expected from his youthfulness, in the tortuous ways of Russian policy and Russian conspiracy, he clearly foresaw that either the Duchess Regent, or the Princess Elizabeth, would be forced into immediate action. To which side should he incline? On the one hand he knew, perhaps better than any other man in St. Petersburg, that the relations between the Duke of Courland and the Princess Elizabeth had always been of an amicable character. Powerful as the Duke's influence had been with the late Empress, it had not been potent enough to guide her entirely as to her conduct towards the other members of the Imperial family. Had it been otherwise, it is by no means improbable that the Princess Elizabeth would, at an early period, have been chosen by the Empress as her successor to the throne,—at a period earlier at least than that when the Czarina began to show favour to the House of Brunswick.

If, therefore, Ivan should make up his mind to betray the plot to the Duchess Regent, he might be greatly injuring the Duke of Courland's interests, and indeed preventing his recall. However much Ivan may have feared his master in former days, and however little he may have trusted the Duke's graciousness, when he was gracious to his private secretary, Ivan thought it would be a sin to be untrue to his master in the days of his adversity.

What effect either course might have upon the fortunes of the Princess Marie's family, he could not determine in his mind. But upon the whole he thought that. any change in the ruling powers could not be unfavourable to them.

On the other hand, gratitude impelled him strongly to take the side of the Duchess Regent, to whose especial kindness he thought he owed his own return from exile.

It is very seldom that any human being, when placed in difficult circumstances, is driven by one single simple motive to adopt a definite course of action. Without in the least detracting from the influence which a feeling of gratitude excited in the mind of this young man, he perhaps might have remained inactive, but for the following consideration. He began to think, as some observers at the time thought, and as many historians since have thought, until they came to the catastrophe, that a plot so weakly contrived, must fail.

" And then," said Ivan to himself, " if I take that side, I shall have gained' no advantage for the Duke of Courland or for my loved friends in Siberia. The thing will fail. I feel almost sure that it will. Did I feel otherwise, I could hardly resolve upon action. A plot known to the gypsies; talked over, for so I can see it is, by those common soldiers at the café, when half drunk; a plot constructed by that gabbling Frenchman, Lestocq!—Count Ostermann must be strangely altered if he fail to find it out. I must be quick, whatever I decide to do."

As he thus reasoned with himself, he arrived at a final result. It was nightfall then; but he resolved to go next morning to the Winter Palace, and to seek an audience with the Duchess Regent.

BOOK III.

———◆———

CHAPTER VI.

MAVRA SCHEPELOF AND HER MISTRESS.

THE chief conspirator, Lestocq, now comes again upon the scene. When last mentioned, he had just returned from his visit to the café, and had entered the palace of the Princess Elizabeth.

In a richly-furnished room of that palace, there sat two ladies. One was a tall and beautiful young woman, with somewhat severe features, of what is called a classical type. She was Mavra Schepelof, the first lady-in-waiting to the Princess Elizabeth, and was greatly be-

loved by her. The other was the Princess
Elizabeth herself. This royal lady is well worth
describing, being a person who played a large
part in the world's history. She was eminently
handsome, having much of the beauty of her
Empress-Mother Catharine, the wife of Peter
the Great. Good humour, voluptuousness, wit
and intellectual ability, were all depicted in her
countenance. It was, however, more marked and
impressive than quite beseems what is most beautiful in woman. Her dress was very remarkable.
She was enveloped in a kind of cloak, trimmed
with lace, as well as with the richest furs.
Had it not been for the lace, you might almost
have supposed it to be a man's cloak; and certainly, whenever the cloak was a little thrown
aside by any gesture more animated than
usual, a mode of attire appeared beneath,
which was, in all respects, decidedly masculine.
She wore a sort of tunic which well became
the outlines of a form which was graceful,
though it must be allowed to have been of rather
too ample a development.

That very day the English ambassador, in writing home to his government, had informed them, that the power of the Duchess Regent was becoming more and more secure. Indeed, he said, there was but little to fear from the Princess Elizabeth, for she was too stout to be a conspirator ; and the ambassador confirmed his opinion by quoting Shakespeare, who also had pronounced that there was little danger to be apprehended from the machinations of fat people.

It may be remarked how much these ambassadors indulge in quotations from Shakespeare—thereby a little contradicting the popular theory, that Addison re-introduced Shakespeare to the English reading world. This ambassador—a man of Addison's own age—was not likely to have been influenced in his early studies by anything that Addison ever wrote.

His Excellency would have been delighted to have overheard the conversation which ensued between these two ladies ; and the despatch which he would afterwards have written, would have contained still more convincing proofs of the permanence of the existing government in Russia.

The conversation of the two ladies had hitherto turned upon somewhat frivolous subjects, such as the dress of the Duchess Regent, of her favourite, Juliana de Mengden, and the presents which had lately been given, in the name of the infant Emperor, to the Princess Elizabeth on her birthday. This talk was interrupted by a knock at the door, when a page entered and said that Monsieur Lestocq desired to have the honour of an audience with her Highness.

"Let him wait," said the Princess; with which message the page retired.

"Do not look so vexed, dear Mavra. I know what the man has come to say. He has said it a hundred times before, as you well know; and I have made the same reply a hundred times."

"Is your Highness then prepared to marry

that hump-backed fright, the Duchess's brother-in-law ? "

" No, dear Mavra, I decline to marry any man, whether he be as frightful as some of my ancestors must have been, if they have not been belied by the Court painters (and that I hardly think is likely), or as beautiful as that Apollo in the corridor. No man shall have it in his power to tyrannize over me."

" Does your Highness mean to endure the slights that are put upon you from day to day by these upstarts—you, the real heiress of Russia ? Do you mean to let all State affairs go on without your having any voice in them ? "

" Mavra, my dear, you should have been the Princess ; and I should have been the first lady-in-waiting. What an Empress, by the way, you would have made ! A good face, too, for a coin ! Here, now, there is some dignity of form and feature."

" Your Highness is pleased to mock me."

" No, my child, I am not mocking you."

"And what a good change it would have been for me — what a lady-in-waiting I should have made! So good humoured, so placable, so easily to be managed by any other woman. Now, Mavra, confess : have I not a better temper than any of you? I should make the Princess of Ladies-in-waiting. I never pout when I am ordered to do anything that is disagreeable— except just a little when I have to go to Court, and play the hypocrite to that stupid woman, and her still more stupid favourite, and to admire, with becoming reverence, that Imperial Infant, 'the sweetest and most intelligent little creature that ever breathed.' "

Here the Princess burst into a hearty masculine kind of laugh, in which her companion did not join.

"And so it won't laugh, won't it? Its head is full of State affairs. State affairs! Mavra, I will tell you a great secret. These State affairs that men talk about are the greatest farce in the world. If men only cared to talk to me about State affairs, I should not care to listen to them so readily as my enemies say that I am prone to do.

"Since my good father's death, the State affairs that seem such grand things to you, have chiefly been, as far as my poor intelligence has discovered, that one great man is sent to Siberia with a round following of his henchmen, and another great man, with his slaves and flatterers, comes up and takes the vacant place. These are great State affairs. But I have forgotten—there are the coats. These garments play a large part in State affairs. Stars and crosses are pulled off certain coats, and are put upon others.

"Believe me, Mavra, there is nothing worth having like a quiet life, with a little love, occasionally, to sweeten it. In love there may be variety, else it becomes a dull affair, to my thinking. Don't look so shocked, my dear : your Feodor and you, are to be changeless turtle-doves, I know, and to coo, and coo, and coo, as unrelentingly as those most tiresome of feathered bipeds."

And this was the woman, speaking at this moment, probably without any disguise, and showing her real character, who afterwards, though reluctantly, kept a great part of Europe in a state of constant turmoil; and whose administration of foreign affairs tended largely to increase and consolidate the power of Russia.

The favourite reminded the Princess that Lestocq was waiting.

"I will see him now, my dear — this great statesman who wishes to administer his potions to the body politic; and is ready to do so with as much confidence in his own skill, and as little fear of consequences, as when he plays the part of doctor to our household. We, however, have seldom cared to avail ourselves of his skill."

"Your Highness must make mirth out of all of us who have the happiness to attend upon you; but I would that you would listen to him *less or more;* for I am sure that you are in great peril while you hesitate. May I leave you ?"

The Princess, with a sigh, gave her consent. Mavra Schepelof withdrew; and shortly afterwards Lestocq entered the apartment.

It was with a very grave aspect and with much reverence that Lestocq approached the Princess, and stood in front of her.

"My good Lestocq," exclaimed the Princess, "are any of your patients recovering from their medicines, that you come hither with such grave and sour looks, which ill become you? What is it, man?"

"All is ready, please your Highness; and when I have said all is ready, it means that there is not a day to be lost. From readiness to ripeness, from ripeness to rottenness, there is but a small interval in these affairs."

"The similitude is not savoury, but the aphorism is worthy of the gravity of the Chancellor himself. You must have been talking lately with the wise Count Ostermann—the man who is always ill at the right time. Cure him of that, Lestocq, cure the fox of his cunning, if you can."

"I should know something about him," Lestocq replied. "I am mostly followed by his spies. But hear me, Princess. Do, for once, hear me, and believe your faithful friend and servant. I have come from the café of the soldiers. Your friends there are most impatient. Grunstein declares that it is madness to wait. La Chétardie says so too."

"France, I know, is deeply interested in the good government of Russia," said the Princess.

"Your partisans, madam, in the Preobraskenski regiment, are devoted to you. But how can you rely for a moment on their prudence? These common fellows must talk.

"And some others too, Lestocq."

"And they have wives and sweethearts."

"Aye: I warrant me they have," said the Princess. "That is not a point upon which I am doubtful."

"And the Cuirassiers are ordered to Sweden. I told you, before, that other regiments had been sent.

"Ha!" exclaimed the Princess, whose coun-

tenance suddenly changed, "that is something
serious. Next to the Preobraskenskis, they are
our best friends. Think you, Lestocq, that that
is the reason why they are sent away from St.
Petersburg ? "

" Not a doubt of it : and, madam, is it not a
childish fancy (if I may say so), which has
fixed upon the 'Consecration of the Waters' as
the day for our attempt, merely because it is a
day of festival, which may serve their purposes
as well as ours ? I do not see why we should
desire to have many people in the streets on
our day. That day must be advanced."

" We will see about it," said the Princess.

Lestocq shrugged his shoulders in a most
emphatic manner, and muttered discontentedly
to himself the Princess's words, " We will see
about it."

" I tell you, Lestocq, I like not the thing. I
marvel at myself that I have ever let you go so
far. It seems a baseness, to be plotting against
this child ; and, as for the woman herself, she

more amuses me than wounds me." Then, after a pause, she said, "To-day I go to Court. I'll mark them well. To-morrow, we will speak further on the matter."

"To-morrow," repeated Lestocq in a mournful tone.

'I would be alone now, Lestocq." So saying she waved her hand gracefully. Lestocq bowed, and withdrew.

He had hardly quitted the room, before the expression of the Princess's face entirely changed. There was now something in it of the stern look of her father : something, too, of the sorrowful look of her mother in her later years. The Princess threw aside the robe which she had kept closely round her while Lestocq was in the room ; and, with slow step, paced up and down the apartment.

The English ambassador might well say, as he does in a letter to his Court, that it would be desirable for the British Government to send the Princess the Order of the Garter, as it would certainly have found a fitting wearer, and would seldom have been seen to more advantage. It was not unwise, too, of the shrewd ambassador to have added, that they had also better send a far better-looking and far younger man than he could pretend to be, to represent them at this Court.

" I like it not," she said; " the more I think of it, the less I like it. I doubt not I could rule a little better than these foolish people; but enough of blood has been shed by our House, and for it. I am not a good woman: at least, according to their empty moralities, I am not such; but I would not have the death of any single human being on my soul. Should I be forced to take this step (and they are all in my power, a word from me condemns them) during my reign there shall be no executions. If tame and uneventful, at any rate it shall be blood- less. Why talk of my reign? I will not reign. We'll see, though; we'll see. If they push me to the precipice, it is not Peter's daughter who will be thrust over it, or not alone, not alone.. They shall all go with me."

The Princess continued for some time muttering indistinct sentences of a similar kind to those which she had spoken loudly; and then, calling for her tiring women, she prepared to attend the Court on a day which proved very eventful as regards the destinies of Russia.

BOOK III.

CHAPTER VII.

THE GRAND DUCHESS HAS A PRIVATE INTERVIEW WITH THE PRINCESS ELIZABETH.

It was a grand day at the Russian Court; and the scene, if not looked at too closely, was magnificent in the extreme. The splendour that the Duke of Courland had introduced, suffered no abatement during the new reign; and the Court presented a very different appearance from that which the Princess Elizabeth had been accustomed to in her early days, during the reign of her rude and boisterous father, Peter the Great.

Even now, however, to the eyes of a fastidious

Frenchman, and many such were present on this occasion, there was much that provoked criticism. There was not anything in all its parts complete. If a man was otherwise well-dressed, that important part of his costume, the wig, was neither what it should have been, nor worn as it should have been. As for the dress of the ladies, the material was often of gold brocade, or of some other rich material; but, as Lestocq did not fail to remark to a compatriot, "there was a total absence of fine feeling in the composition. No poetry whatever!" A colour endurable enough in itself, though rather pronounced, was insulted by being placed in juxtaposition with some other bold colour, which could not possibly live on good terms with it. "And then the walk of the women! Only to be equalled in barbarism by the brutal manner in which the men thump their diamond snuff-boxes, and take snuff like clowns."

Such were the biting remarks of Lestocq, who almost felt that it was beneath his genius to concern himself with the politics of a people vainly

endeavouring, as he said to himself, to conceal
their native savagery by this awkward splendour. " The wolves wear the ermine they have
stolen ; but when the creatures move or utter
sounds, the wolf in them is not less visible."

It was the custom at that Court for members of the Imperial Family to be received at
their entrance by a flourish of trumpets. This
was not omitted on the present occasion when
the Princess Elizabeth entered the Winter Palace ; and, indeed, she was received with marked
cordiality by the Duchess Regent and her husband, the Grand Duke of Brunswick.

After the Princess had remained a short time
in the circle, the Duchess Regent suddenly made
a sign to her ; and they withdrew together from
the drawing-room to the Grand Duchess's private
apartments.

It was with very anxious feelings that Lestocq,
the French ambassador, La Chétardie, and
Woronzkow saw this movement of those two
great personages. These men were the only
persons present who were thoroughly aware how

far the Princess had gone in conspiracy, or at least in allowing conspiracy in her behalf, against the reigning powers.

The step thus taken by the Grand Duchess, of withdrawing herself and the Princess from the Court circle was a most unusual one; and, as to a conspirator even very slight circumstances are matters of no light concern, such an event at Court as this, was calculated to excite the most serious apprehensions in the minds of the guilty persons present.

When the two ladies had entered the Duchess Regent's cabinet, she lost no time in taxing the Princess with her conduct. The Regent told her frankly that, from various quarters, information had reached her of the Princess's proceedings. Lestocq, a member of her household, was in constant communication with the French ambassador; and it was well known that those two were carrying on the most dangerous intrigues. Hitherto, she, the Regent, had refused to give any credence to the information she had received; but if these treasonable practices continued, Lestocq must be arrested, and means would be taken to make him confess the truth.

The Princess in reply showed a power of dissembling which proved that she was well fitted to take a high position in that political world of dissimulation, in the midst of which she lived. She was innocence itself. Had she ever shown any ambitious desires? Nothing was further from her thoughts than to do anything which could injure the Duchess Regent, or that dear child, the infant Emperor. She trusted that she had too deep a sense of religion to break the oath of fealty she had taken. As for Lestocq, he had never entered the French Ambassador's Palace. This statement was true to the letter; for, as it may be remembered, he had always carefully avoided doing so. However, the Princess added, Lestocq might be arrested if the Regent pleased. What he would confess, if he spoke truly, would only place his mistress's innocence in a stronger light. For her part, she knew that she had enemies, and that all these

stories against her were told by them, in order
to make her life miserable at Court.

While uttering these protestations she was
deeply affected, and shed abundant tears. The
good-natured Grand Duchess wept in sympathy ; ·
and the two great ladies returned into the
drawing-room : the one believing that she had
been listening to the reclamations of an innocent
person who had been most wrongfully accused,
and the other feeling that she had played her
part of innocence very well ; but that it could
not often be played again. Moreover, she had
that almost sickening sensation of great fear
which comes upon most persons, when, by the
merest hazard, or by great skill, a sudden danger has just been avoided by them, at which
moment the sense of peril is perhaps the
greatest.

BOOK III.

CHAPTER VIII.

PROGRESS OF THE CONSPIRACY.

WHEN the two great ladies returned to the drawing-room, it was with arms inter-linked, and seemingly in very loving converse with each other. It is almost needless to add that the eyes of every courtier were directed, either openly or furtively, to the countenances of the Princess and the Duchess Regent.

Even false tears leave distinct traces on the countenance; and that composure of mind, which enabled the Princess to command the expression of every feature, did not enable her to remove those tell-tale signs of recent tears, which betrayed the serious and affecting nature of the interview.

In a few moments it was thoroughly well known by experienced Russian courtiers, what kind of scene had been enacted. Those among them who had some inkling of the designs of the two chief conspirators, Lestocq and La Chétardie, quickly turned their eyes from the countenances of the ladies, to the faces of these two men. They bore the inspection very well. The native gaiety of these two Frenchmen almost baffled, for the moment, the searching inquiries which were directed, not only to their looks, but to their whole demeanour.

It was a terrible evening for the Princess Elizabeth. Years afterwards she remembered how she had thought that the festivities of that night would never end. At last, however, they did end; and, after an affectionate parting with the Duchess Regent, the Princess, accompanied by her suite, returned to her own palace.

The suite, with one exception, were immediately dismissed; and then the Princess, beckoning Lestocq to accompany her, retired to her private apartments.

To him the Princess related, without reserve, all that had passed between her and the Duchess Regent. In the midst of her own terror and perplexity, she could not help being somewhat amused by the much greater terror manifested by Lestocq, especially when the Princess related to him how the Duchess Regent had intimated that it might be necessary to arrest Lestocq, and to ascertain that which torture might compel him to confess.

Lestocq, as might be imagined, was for instant action. He was very bold, intellectually speaking, as a conspirator; but that is by no means inconsistent with his having a very sincere and careful regard for the welfare of his own person. He was a little shocked, too, at finding that the Princess had made no objection whatever to his being arrested, and had, in fact, consented that this arrest should take place. It was in vain that the Princess pointed out to him that any hesitation at that moment would have been absolutely fatal—would, in fact, have caused the instant death or banishment to Siberia, of all persons who were directly, or even remotely, concerned in this conspiracy—a conspiracy which had been so carelessly, and, if we may so express it, so disrespectfully conducted, that it might almost have been termed " an open secret."

To all Lestocq's lamentations and entreaties —entreaties for instant action, that very night— the Princess paid no heed. Her simple reply was, " The good woman is sufficiently imposed upon by the bad woman, so far at any rate that the effect may be expected to last for the next twenty-four hours. Leave me, leave me now," she exclaimed, " I will not resolve to-night what shall be done. To-morrow, come early : there shall be no more hesitation after this night. But now, go."

Lestocq, though with a very unwilling mind, left the apartment.

It was a terrible night that the Princess passed

on this occasion.   Naturally of an indecisive tem-
perament— of an easy-going, indolent, voluptuous
disposition—and having only dormant in her the
restless energy of that most restless of monarchs,
her Father :—she had, hitherto, only played with
this conspiracy.   True it is, she had been vexed
by the slights which she had met with, or fancied
she had met with, at the hands of the new
reigning powers.   Moreover, it had been a
serious grievance to her, that she should have
been much pressed to marry the insignificant and
deformed brother of the Duchess Regent's
husband.   This pressure was the more distasteful
to her, as she was not without lovers, whom she
regarded, according at least to the scandal of the
Court, with exceeding favour.   She, however,
knew that the people of Russia would never
allow the daughter of Peter the Great to be
forced into a marriage which was entirely re-
pugnant to her, and which was so obviously
meant to secure the interests of a German
family, not at all too much loved either by the
nobles or the common people of Russia.

The religious difficulty, however, was the one which weighed most with the Princess, through-out that anxious and sleepless night. She had sworn an oath of fealty to the infant Emperor; and whatever follies, or whatever severities the Duchess Regent might commit, either against herself, or against those who were devoted to her Imperial Highness, this oath that she had solemnly and deliberately taken, being perfectly aware of how much of her own rights she had given up by taking it, weighed upon her con-science.

It needs but little knowledge of history, to be convinced of the fact that religion may not relax its hold upon those persons, who seem the most to contradict its teachings. The Princess, was, doubtless, a most erring woman; and, with that singular candour of character which she possessed, she was but too well aware that she contradicted some of the ordinary precepts of morality. But, she ever held, that in matters of religion, she was a true and faithful servant of the Church. In the breast of such an orthodox and dutiful believer,

what excuse could there be for perjury? Moreover, there seemed to her something very mean
in conspiring against a mere child. She was ex-
ceedingly fond of children; and, though she
ridiculed at times to her dependants the almost
ludicrous devotion of the Regent Mother, and of
the whole Court to the little Ivan, the Princess
had been fond of the child, and had been quite
contented to abide the time, sixteen years hence,
when he would be called to ascend the throne,
and take the reins of government into his own
hands. The people at present in power, she
despised. The very conquest she had made, this
evening, over the just fears of the Duchess Regent,
had not diminished her contempt for that good-
natured lady; but, at the same time, had made
the Princess feel how inglorious a thing it would
be to supplant this good, innocent woman by
sheer treason. The Princess imagined that she
herself had no especial capacity for governing.
How greatly this inadequate knowledge of her
own powers would be contradicted, remained to
be seen.

The result was, that the night was passed by
her in stating and re-stating every conceivable
argument that should induce her to decide one
way or the other.   Should she go at once to the
Duchess Regent ; acknowledge frankly the extent
to which the conspiracy had proceeded ; claim
pardon for Lestocq, immunity for the French
ambassador, La Chétardie ; and, then, as it were,
disband the conspirators ?   This was one course
of action to which her thoughts inclined.

She felt, though, that for such a course to be
successful, it was requisite that the other side
should be equally generous with herself.   It was
characteristic of her sagacity, that she said to
herself : " Small-minded people never understand
large-hearted conduct ; aud they will still continue
to suspect me, however innocent I may be."

Finally, she resolved to determine nothing
until she should again see, or hear from, those
who were considered to be her friends in St
Petersburg.

The Princess was right in supposing that she
had twenty-four hours of safety.   She had played

her dissembling part so well that the Duchess Regent was perfectly convinced of her innocence. It was in vain that the Grand Duke endeavoured that very evening to persuade his wife to consent to the arrest of Lestocq, and to post additional piquets in the streets.

It is clear that the system of placing piquets in the streets, the abolition of which had given so much satisfaction when the Duke of Courland was deposed, had again been introduced, though probably not to so great an extent as in his time.

BOOK III.

——◆——

CHAPTER IX.

LESTOCQ'S FINAL INTERVIEW WITH THE PRINCESS
ELIZABETH.

THE next morning, very early, Lestocq
claimed an interview with the Princess. His
fears throughout that night, had not by any
means diminished. Visions of the knout and the
rack had come most painfully before him. He
knew full well that he was not one of that " noble
army of martyrs," whom torture does not compel
to betray their secrets, or even the secrets of other
people. Indeed, it is very rare that any motive,
other than that afforded by the solemn duty of

holding to a religious belief, enables any man to
endure the torments of skilled torture without
renouncing the most cherished convictions, or
betraying the most secret knowledge possessed
by him.

At first, the conversation of this morning was
very like that of the preceding evening. Lestocq urged immediate action. The Princess
contended against his views. If action were to
be taken, why not keep to their original plan,
and choose the festival of the " Consecration of
the Waters of the Neva " as the day on which
the conspiracy should break forth ?

" You say," exclaimed the Princess, " and
perhaps it is true, that I am beloved by the
troops : you say, and I do not deny it, that I am
beloved by the people. Then and there we can
best learn whether their love for me is such as
would, with the consent of all, place me upon the
throne of my father."

As may be seen, the horrible state of indecision in which this great Princess had passed the
night, still remained dominant upon her. She

well knew that she was surrounded by adventurers. They risked but their bodies : she felt, devout as she really was, that she risked her soul. As a politician, thoroughly conversant with the intrigues of foreign courts, she knew that it was from no love of her that France, through her ambassador, was a most willing party to this conspiracy. Even at this supreme moment of her fortunes, she resolved that if she committed this great treason, it should not, after all, prove so very beneficial to the intrigues of Louis XV. "What do they seek," she exclaimed, "but to prolong our intestine discord, and to make Russia powerless, and France predominant in the affairs of Europe ? "

Cardinal Fleury, and his master Louis, would little have liked to see the severe smile which lightened up the face of the Princess, when she was thinking over the part which they so gladly played, and with such lavish expenditure of money, solely to embarrass her dear Russia, to which by so many ties of filial affection, she was entirely devoted.

Meanwhile, during the time that these thoughts and others, some more worthy, some less worthy of a great mistress of state-craft, were occupying her mind, Lestocq went on talking. He reiterated his own fears, his dread of Ostermann and Botta, who could not be cajoled as the Duchess Regent had been ; the impatience of the common soldiery, who were devoted to her cause, and whom he had met with at the café of the Preobraskenski regiment on the preceding evening.

Gradually, during this animated interview, in which, however, Lestocq had taken the principal part, and the answers of the Princess had chiefly been confined to a simple ' Yes ' or ' No ; ' and indeed to which she had sometimes not deigned to make any answer whatever, he had broken through the usual severe forms of Russian etiquette at Court, and had finally taken his seat at the table at which the Princess Elizabeth was sitting. It chanced that on that table lay a large piece of cardboard. The Princess was an artist herself, as well as a great encourager of

art; and this cardboard was probably put out for
some drawing that she was to make.   It was,
however, destined for a greater purpose than any
drawing that any Princess, even one so accomplished as Elizabeth of Russia, could design.

Lestocq, who was an abundant talker, the
vainest of men, continued to urge, in various
forms of words, the various arguments which
have hitherto been stated.   At the same time he
was very busy with his pencil, for he was an admirable draughtsman.   The Princess was somewhat amused with the whole proceeding, especially with Lestocq's audacity in seating himself
at the same table with her.   If she had been
asked what she thought he was doing, she would
most likely have answered that he was caricatur-
ing, for she knew his skill and wit in that dangerous art,—that he was perhaps depicting the
scene at the Russian Court of yesterday,
and that she was to appear disfigured by her
tears after her interview with the Duchess
Regent.

The conversation languished, and by way of

continuing it, she asked him to show her what he had been drawing. The result rather surprised her. He had made an admirable likeness of herself, clad in the robes of a sovereign of Russia, with a crown upon her head. This drawing occupied one half of one side of the cardboard. On the other, she appeared in the dress of a nun, with a very deplorable countenance, rendered very thin by mortification and fasting, and affording a ludicrous contrast to the genial, jovial face, which her Imperial Highness was wont to show to the common soldiers, whom she allowed to get up behind her sledge, and to accompany her through the streets of St. Petersburg, such favoured individuals being considered by common consent, and without much reproach, to be her favoured lovers.

On the other side of the cardboard were depicted Lestocq himself, and other accomplices, enduring the torments of the rack.

It was surprising to see the effect which these drawings produced upon the Princess Elizabeth. She looked at the cardboard fixedly. She turned it over and over again several times, regarding, with stern contemplation, its rude portraitures, which were not without considerable pictorial merit. Never did any work of any artist, not of a Michael Angelo, a Titian or a Murillo, have such direct effect upon the destinies of the world.

The Princess whispered a few words to Lestocq; but they appeared to be most decisive words, for an expression of gladness pervaded his countenance, and he quitted the room hastily and abruptly.

Three minutes had not elapsed before the Princess summoned her attendants, and desired that instant search should be made for Lestocq, and that he should be recalled to her presence. But no one could find him. He had left the palace : no one could tell whither he had gone. And thus that final moment of indecision, for indecision it doubtless was, had no effect; and the Princess was irretrievably bound to whatever course she had decided to take, in the few brief whispers (for conspirators speak in whispers even when they are in their secret chambers and fear no spies,) which she had exchanged with Lestocq, after a full and earnest contemplation of those rude drawings which appeared to have excelled in eloquence all speech.

END OF VOL. I.

PRINTED BY TAYLOR AND CO.,
LITTLE QUEEN STREET, LINCOLN'S INN FIELDS.